"I never wanted you to know about the dreams," Etan said. "I feel crazy enough without you confirming it."

"Crazy isn't the question," Alex said, stroking Etan's hair. "Unless it's both of us. You missed me saying every word feels *true*."

"I don't even know what the dreams are, Alex. I know I have them, but I never remember a thing. That's not exactly stable."

"Well, have a drink and let me enlighten you."

Etan sat up, managing to keep himself from curling up into a knot of fear again. He drained the whiskey, watching Alex do the same.

"What you tell me in the middle of the night is all about how we can't stay here much longer. Something bad is going to happen, with the food supply I think, and none of the cities are going to be safe anymore. And we don't have much time to get ready before we're trapped along with everyone else who's not going to make it out."

For Jason

*Who knows what it's like to leave the mountains
and to come back home.*

JOINING THE STORM

BOOK TWO OF THE STORMS OF FUTURE PAST SERIES

KARI KILGORE

SPIRAL PUBLISHING, LTD.

Chapter 1

Alex Collins was never asleep when he was supposed to be. His parents gave up trying to hide holiday gifts or replace his lost teeth with money before he turned five. He was the kind of kid who didn't care for surprises anyway. He preferred to know what lay ahead of him. By the time his brother and sister were old enough to consider sneaking out of the house at night, they already knew it would be pointless.

Life on the outskirts Fond du Lac, Wisconsin, gave Alex the stability he craved. Giggling about the French translation of Fond du Lac as *Bottom of the Lake* before he even started school gave him the first taste of the humor that would always sustain him.

He saw patterns all around him. The orderly grids of streets, noises and bursts of activity with shift changes at factories, migrations of huge flocks of birds each spring and fall. All gave him the framework he needed to withstand the upheavals of childhood.

In the summer of his thirteenth year, the comfort of routine failed him. Patterns transformed into prison bars, hemming him in, dragging him inexorably onto a path no one around him thought to question. An approved set of classes in high school would lead to community college, then to the University of Wisconsin and a solid, respectable corporate job shuffling papers in Madison or Milwaukee.

He could detour into the factory, like his father. Or the farm, like his grandfather.

Either way, Alex knew he would sink into oblivion and disappear.

Around the same time, the fundamental honesty that kept him from pretending he didn't know about his parents' late night activities drove an impenetrable wedge through the middle of his family.

Alex wasn't quite old enough to know he should pretend he didn't notice when certain patterns changed.

Distance between him and his father grew first, and most painfully. Seeing the changes, less time spent together, avoiding Alex's activities, and more harsh words than kind, didn't help him understand what was going wrong. One conversation brought more clarity than anyone wanted.

Glen Collins had picked all of them up from school for the third time that week, a task he'd rarely done before the past several weeks. Alex sat at the desk in the den, while his brother and sister sat with his father on the sectional sofa lining three walls of the carpeted basement space.

The other kids had their mother's straight blond hair, and Alex had red like his father, just starting to curl enough to be horribly unruly.

Nearly as unruly as his mouth sometimes.

"Did Mom get a different job?" Alex said.

"No, son. She's had the same job for seven years now. You know that."

Alex looked up from his math homework, warning prickling along his spine. His father didn't sound annoyed as he had so often lately. He sounded afraid.

"I just thought..." he said, not sure how to make everything better but needing to. "So many things have changed over the past couple of months. That's all."

His father shut down his reader with an ominous sigh. He lowered his chin and looked at Alex.

"Is that so? Why don't you enlighten me about all these changes?"

Alex was scared he wouldn't be able to answer through a dry throat and mouth. His after school sandwich weighed heavily in his belly.

"That's okay, Dad."

"No, it's not." The other two kids were ignoring their own homework now, watching the exchange. "You're always so full of information, noticing every little thing, whether we want it or not. Well, I want it. Start talking. Now."

"You pick us up more," Alex said, forcing the words out. "So I thought she was working late more. She bought a bunch of new clothes. I wondered if they made her wear different stuff. And with her new haircut, I thought she seemed happier or something."

"New haircut," his father said. He sat back and crossed his arms. "That it?"

An alarm deep in Alex's brain, triggered by budding empathy or self-preservation, kept him silent.

"Know what I think, Alex? I think I've had just about enough of your vivid imagination and your little games. Next time you have a bunch of lies and nonsense you just have to tell someone, save it for school. Or for your mother."

"Dad, I didn't mean to upset you," Alex said. "I'm not imagining things. I'm not lying. I feel like something *good* is going to happen to Mom, not something bad."

This time the flash of fear and fury in his father's eyes made Alex cringe in the hard wooden chair.

"What are you doing, making notes of her movements? Spying on us? Do your damn homework! I don't want to hear another word. In fact, why don't you take yourself and your excess of attention up to your room?"

Alex gathered up his things, heart pounding in his throat, tears in his eyes. Worse than his father's shout was the fear he'd clearly seen in his brother and sister. They both drew away, faces pale and eyes wide.

When his mother got home two hours later, he heard more shouting that didn't stop until his mother talked to him a week later. She walked into his room looking sad and exhausted.

"Listen, Alex. I don't know what you told your father. But I'm not sick, losing my job, or having an affair. I've been going for a promotion, which I may not get after the last week of going to work asleep on my feet."

"I wasn't trying to cause trouble," Alex said, trying not to cry. "I just noticed something was different. I thought it was going to be something good."

"Well, it may still be if I can make up for the past few days." She rubbed her eyes, then looked at Alex again. Her brown eyes were red around the edges. "I know you think you see a lot of things, and sometimes you probably do. You're not old enough to know when to keep your mouth shut. Do me a favor, kiddo. Don't be on my side."

FROM THAT DAY ON, the patterns around Alex shifted. Instead of a safety net or a constricting trap, he saw a way forward. A way to move. His inner eye followed sidewalks, roads, even plants that leaned away from the lake he'd grown up at the bottom of.

Alex's mind, and his heart, were set on a path to the southeast.

He got into the habit of keeping quiet and keeping his head down at home. That routine left him lonely, but he was grateful for the calm. At school, though, he embraced the opposite and excelled beyond his own vague ambitions of living somewhere else. His love of math and the sure answers it provided refined into a passion, as did his perhaps less endearing habit of taking apart everything mechanical he could get his hands on.

People in Alex's life, even his parents, eventually stopped worrying about finding their belongings in pieces. He always managed to put things back together. And they often worked better than they had before.

His calculus teacher called him aside in the middle of his junior year. Ms. Powers was the best teacher Alex had had so far, challenging and pushing him beyond what even he thought he could do.

"So what are you planning to do once you get out of here, Alex?"

she said. She was perched on her desk, swinging her sneaker-clad feet like a kid.

"You mean today? Or after next year?"

"I mean next year," she said, smiling. "Today's all up to you, though I know you'll get your work done before Monday. What are your plans for college?"

Alex kicked at the tile floor, then tried to disappear into himself when his shoe made an obnoxious shriek.

"Community college for a couple of years, I guess. I don't know after that. Maybe the math department down in Madison."

"That's a perfectly sensible plan," she said. "And I know you can do better. Is any of that what you *want* to do? Do you want to teach?"

"I think it's what I *can* do. I don't love the idea of teaching, but we're not exactly rich."

Alex didn't say what he was really thinking. He hadn't had any big outbursts with his parents for the last couple of years. But he doubted sending their strange and overly observant son to a hugely expensive school right away was high on the list. Even with that big promotion his mother had earned after all.

"Well, I'd like to talk to a few people," Ms. Powers said, "but I wanted to talk to you first. You don't have to teach, Alex, though I think you'd be pretty good at it. I've seen you tutor more than one kid who was struggling. Do me a favor. Take some time over the weekend and look into engineering. With what I hear about the way you run circles around everyone else in your industrial shop class, you'd be a natural. The teachers are afraid you'll go through all their projects before the end of the semester."

"I am a little bored in there," Alex said before he stopped to think. He felt his face and ears blazing hot. "Please don't tell them I said that."

"No, that's what *they're* telling me." Ms. Powers was smiling, not scolding. "There are some fine schools here, but I have one in mind where a friend from my college days teaches."

Alex closed his eyes, waiting for the odd shockwave moving through him to subside. He saw all the decisions, small and large, leading to this moment. Doubling up on math for the past two years. Asking for extra work whenever he could.

Making sure he got into *this* class, correctly rumored to be tougher than the other two.

He didn't have to ask, but Alex knew he should. No one else knew about the patterns, the way motion and arrangement and confluence directed and shaped his life. That was best kept to himself.

"Where is it?"

"Chicago. Not too far from home, is it?"

Alex laughed, looking down at his feet to hide the quick tears in his eyes. The map resolved in his head, with his home at the bottom of a much bigger lake.

And himself in the middle of a much bigger life.

"Not too far at all, Ms. Powers. Not even close."

Chapter 2

Alex opened his apartment door to a blowing Chicago snowstorm, drifts he didn't want to deal with already building up on the concrete steps. Four people barely recognizable through heavy coats and scarves stared up at him. He'd seen two of them in considerably less clothing a few times over the past five years

"You're not honestly expecting me to go out in this?" he said, holding the door open.

A party had sounded like a good idea a few hours ago, before a blizzard settled in like a heavy blanket over his shoulders. They stomped enthusiastically before stepping inside.

"What exciting plans did you have instead?" said Kim, one of those friends he'd spent close personal time with. "Reading some journal, or working?"

"Neither, thank you very much," Alex said, kissing her cheek. "Just finished up work a few minutes ago. I had plans to watch a shitty movie and go to bed. That's what we do out here in the real world."

"For fuck's sake, Grampa Collins." That was another of Alex's more intimate friends, Thom. "You graduated college early. You didn't magically accelerate to fifty years old."

"Maybe not, but this isn't my crowd anymore. Seriously. Have a couple here if you want, but I'm going to sit this one out."

Kim and the other two, recent dates for his friends who Alex didn't know very well yet, shook their heads and headed back toward the kitchen to take him up on the offer. Thom crossed his arms and stared at Alex with his head tilted.

"I'm afraid I'm going to have to insist you get the hell out of here tonight," he said. "You have the rest of your life to work yourself into a rut like everyone else. And you need to act your age whether you want to or not."

"What am I supposed to talk to them about, Thom? Yeah, I'm still a kid, but I'm not drowning in finals anymore. I'm drowning in work. There's a major conversational disconnect there."

"How about you stop drowning, then, at least for one night?" Thom stepped forward and kissed Alex, hard and deep, cold hands slipping into his hair. He stepped back, grinning. "Just have some fun, man. You still remember how to do that, right? And unless there's someone I don't know about, it's been a while since you got laid. If we're both bored at this party, fine. We head back here and take care of that."

Alex looked around the space, a far cry from the cramped dorm he'd endured with three other guys for three years. This apartment wasn't huge, but it was all his. It did look like a guy in his thirties lived here.

An actual *adult*, one he didn't often feel like.

No evidence of secondhand furniture or dirty clothes, no trace of stale beer or piles of books. He was damn proud of accomplishing so much so young, of getting himself out of his hometown and his parents' house and into a great job.

And Alex wasn't quite ready to join his father's demographic before he turned twenty-three.

He'd been feeling strange and out of sorts all day, off track somehow. That kiss felt pretty fucking good, and it had been a while.

"All right, I'm in. We'll see about your generous offer depending on how the party goes. You and I are great at that part, not so much at the rest."

"Who said anything about the rest?" Thom said, walking toward the kitchen. "I'm planning to use you for your body."

"Works for me. I'll get my coat."

The first steps into the bitter cold nearly sent Alex right back inside. The wind was vicious, driving stinging snow into his face and eyes. Walking two blocks to a college party hoping for some kind of hookup felt like insanity at the moment, but not quite as pathetic as going to bed at nine on a Friday night.

The cars outside the building were already covered with snow. A thick trail of footprints showed the way through the tree-lined courtyard to the second apartment on the left. Alex again considered going back home despite the promise of time with Thom, or someone else. The drifts would surely be up past his knees in a few hours with the way this storm felt.

Alex blinked, sure his eyes were watering from the icy assault. He stopped on the sidewalk, looking back toward the street. That wind had died down inside the sheltered courtyard, leaving the snow to float rather than being driven through a howling tunnel.

Everything he saw, everything he felt, resolved into massive, interlocking patterns.

The streetlight caught the huge flakes and threw sparkling light across several inches on the ground, all lining up to point toward where he stood.

In a lifetime of sensing and feeling such things, he'd never imagined his entire life turning on one point, one moment he did not yet understand. As if a thousand train tracks from all over the world joined in this one spot, then continued on their way.

"Alex is in danger of abandoning us," Kim said from beside him. "He's staring wistfully toward his shitty movie and his bed."

"His *empty* bed," Thom said. "Get your fine ass in gear, old man. I'm freezing mine off out here." He squeezed Alex's backside and pushed, bringing them all in the door laughing.

The heat from an overachieving fireplace and way too many bodies hit Alex like a steaming hot shower while he was fully dressed. There wasn't enough room to stand, much less walk around. And still that movement forward, people shifting to give him a path when there shouldn't be space for one, Thom close behind him, no longer grabbing his ass but adding to the momentum.

Alex looked up, in the direction nothing less than what felt like orbital mechanics was pulling him. He saw one face out of dozens. One man with lovely green eyes, dark brown hair, and the sexiest smile he'd ever seen.

The crowd closed behind him, and Alex walked forward, pulling his coat off. Some part of him knew the years before and the years that would come after still existed. Other people, far too many of them, still lived and breathed all around him.

None of that mattered. This was the moment his whole life, all the choices and hard work and random events, would turn upon.

Alex stepped into his future.

Chapter 3

IN AN INSTANT, in one flash of warm blue eyes, Etan's entire life
made sense.

The party itself was depressingly typical. Far too many college
students jammed into a Chicago courtyard apartment, music too
loud, temperature too high despite heavy snow falling outside. Inex-
pertly rolled joints passed around as easily as fake phone numbers.

Second-hand clothing dragged back from the early decades of
the twenty-first century, styles of their grandparents brought back
from the dead. Every conversation competing to be the most important, the most revolutionary, and the loudest of all time.

Etan desperately needed a break from the toughest bunch of
biology and math classes he'd been foolish enough to take in an indi-
gestible lump, but he only went along to these nightmarish events
out of a sense of obligation. If he'd wanted to sit in his own lonely
shoebox apartment every night, why bother moving to such a huge
city in the first place?

He could have easily taken most of his non-laboratory classes
online for a lot less hard-earned money, even with the huge help of
his grandfather's faculty tuition rate. And he could have stayed in
Southwestern Virginia for all the rest, holed up in the mountains
and living rent-free with his family.

And he would have long since dropped out, or dropped dead, from the never-ending routine and depression.

Etan forced himself to walk through the mob again, escaping the living room with its ear-splitting cheap stereo, broiling fireplace, and shocking chill every time the front door opened. Kitchen followed dining room on the way to bedrooms, all with too many people trying to get a warm body into the closest thing to a bed before they all disappeared into finals.

Several attractive guys and a couple of adventurous girls made it clear Etan was what they were looking for, or at least close enough for the night. Most of the time, he would have taken the chance, if nothing else to get the hell out of the crowd.

With the guys at least. Girls were an unknown territory, one he was more than a little bit afraid of.

He could have even stayed in Appalachia for the casual hookups. Just trade the pretentious wannabe artists for a bunch of grumpy high tech and tourism workers, most of the marijuana for tobacco, and self-conscious wine drinking for cases of nasty beer, and he'd be right back at home. Out in the open or furtive and sneaky, partners were around.

Going home alone, an option too many of the kids in either place seemed afraid of with so much pressure building up as the semester wound down, didn't bother Etan most of the time. The temptation to just say a quick goodbye and disappear was familiar and comfortable to him. He'd stayed a couple of hours longer than he'd planned to already.

Something was different tonight.

Since he was a little boy, Etan had felt a curious sense of dislocation. Hardly anything or anybody around him seemed to fit, and not a damn thing inside of him did. Only his grandparents and father made him feel at home and comfortable.

Part of the trick was they listened to him without trying to convince him he was imagining things. Being around them made him feel like all the sharp and jagged parts of himself at least kept still for a time instead of trying to slice him to ribbons.

As he'd grown up, once in a while he felt one of those parts slip into place. A tiny bit of the noise inside softened, quieted, fell into tune with a song he did not yet recognize. Minor changes like taking his first science class or kissing a guy for the first time, big changes like deciding to go to college so far away from home.

The relief of that smooth internal shift instead of relentless grinding gears let Etan know he was on the right track every time.

And every time, he had a feeling of oncoming alignment, an eclipse in slow motion in his chest. Perhaps a piece he never knew was missing completed several others. Maybe another that hadn't been meant for him in the first place slipped away.

Or simply a part of Etan that had always been used the wrong way, by himself or someone else, fell into perfect motion at last.

Walking around that overheated party in the middle of an early December Illinois snowstorm, he felt the adjustment long before he understood why. The rolling heat throughout his body told him this would be nothing less than fundamental. A change to last the rest of his life.

A burst of laughter from the living room brought a real smile to his face, easing muscles strained from faking for hours. He turned to see a crowd of men and women filtering into the few remaining open spaces.

Flowing into human eddies and currents.

The tides within Etan surged and roared.

One man looked back into his eyes instead of dodging forward to find the alcohol. Snow glittered in curly red hair that brushed his shoulders, with blue eyes framed by a neatly trimmed dark red beard. He smiled at Etan, a friendly, open smile, not the blatant come-ons he'd tried not to return all night long.

This man showed no signs of fear or arrogance, not even a trace of the desperation filling the room as people paired up and departed. Only a confidence too natural to be any kind of act.

And those gorgeous dark blue eyes that made Etan's knees weak. The man walked forward, slipping his heavy black wool jacket off.

"I'm roasting in this thing," he said, his deep voice setting off resonance waves in Etan's stomach. "Know where the standard coat pile is?"

"Not really. I left mine in the car."

"You're a braver man than me, driving tonight," he said, brushing the snow from his hair. "It's really coming down out there."

"I had a feeling it would be worth it." Etan's heart sped up, and he hoped his cheeks weren't turning red.

"Were you right?"

"Not til just now," he said, holding out his hand. "I'm Etan Griffith."

"Alex Collins."

Everything grew from that one warm touch.

Chapter 4

A STRONG GRIP on Alex's hand woke him from a light sleep, all he seemed to manage when he stayed with Etan. The room was still dark, with no sounds of traffic outside the windows. He thought for a second, trying to remember where they'd gone to bed.

Etan's place, that was it. He'd been looking forward to that breathtaking lake view early in the morning.

Not quite *this* early.

Etan's whole body jerked against Alex's back, and he let out a hard breath against his neck. Etan seemed to dream constantly, almost from the second he closed his eyes, but it hadn't been quite this noticeable before.

Alex thought about checking the time, but he didn't want to move far enough to pick up his watch. Etan's apartment was always cold, for one thing, and he had no desire to stir even an inch from their warm bed.

He had the strangest feeling Etan was supposed to have these dreams uninterrupted.

That didn't make a lot of sense, especially if they woke Alex, but that didn't change his certainty. He'd always been a light sleeper anyway, easily able to drop back off.

"Air," Etan said, his voice breathy and higher than normal. "It's in the air. The water. The earth."

He squeezed Alex's hand, curled against his stomach under Etan's, hard enough to hurt. Etan's breathing sped up, and his legs twitched like he was running.

"That doesn't sound like a good one," Alex said under his breath.

He turned over, shifting his grip until he was holding Etan's hand. Strange feeling about letting the dreams go on or not, Alex hated the thought of him being so upset.

"Etan. It's okay. You're just having a dream."

Etan groaned low in his throat, twitching all over now. Alex leaned over him and turned on the dim bedside light.

"Wake up, Etan. Everything's fine."

He could see his boyfriend's face in the light, and Alex drew back in surprise. Etan's eyes were wide open, but they didn't seem to be focusing on him or anything else.

"Everybody dies," he said in a voice that sounded younger, like a little boy's. "No matter what we do, how far we run, everybody dies."

Alex was covered in chills worse than the temperature in the room could explain. That may have sounded like a child's voice, but it didn't sound like a dream voice.

It sounded like the truth.

"Why do they die?" he whispered.

"Poison in the air. Poison in the water. Murder in their hearts. Everybody dies." Etan's voice trailed off on the last two words, and Alex's hair stood on end.

"What can we do about it, E?"

He touched Etan's sweaty cheek, not sure if he wanted to wake him or let the unnerving conversation continue.

"Have to go. Can't stay here." Etan's eyes were squinting but still open, and the edges of his mouth drew down.

"Where do we have to go?"

"Southeast. Our future lies southeast."

Alex closed his eyes, his own body clammy with sweat now. He'd seen that same direction leading him out of Fond du Lac five years before, into this city he loved, a job he loved almost as much. Most importantly into this warm bed with Etan, and a passion and connection he'd never even daydreamed about.

Etan's body went rigid, then he sighed in that same high voice. He turned over, moving back against Alex's chest. His breathing dropped to calm and regular right away, the same rhythm he kept until morning.

Alex knew Etan didn't dream again because he watched for the rest of the night.

His certainty about the solid permanence of their lives together, built into his internal foundation barely six months after they'd met, withstood a serious blow with that first speaking dream.

Alex's foundation wouldn't shatter and collapse until almost three years later.

HE MOVED into Etan's nighttime routine as easily as he had his daytime one. Alex went to sleep a couple of hours before, claiming the early hours of an old working man forced him to. He really wanted to get as much sleep as he could before the dreams started.

He woke a few minutes before, keeping track of the time night after night. He started wearing his wristwatch to bed to make that easier without waking his lover. Three seventeen, three twenty, never later than three thirty. Over and over again.

If Etan slept for more than a few more minutes past that internal alarm, Alex knew he'd sleep right through the night. More than half the time, he opened his eyes and the eerie conversation started.

Etan dreamed of the problem with everyone dying most often, but other patterns emerged as the months and years passed.

Alex tried to ignore the first one that concerned him, tried to pretend it was just a normal dream that didn't mean anything. He was still unsurprised when he got laid off from his first job out of college. It hurt even with the warning, but the disappointment was tempered by awe.

Alex knew when his sister was going to call with news of her marriage, and very shortly thereafter, her pregnancy. Same with family members who died. Knowing he'd have a much better job with a great engineering firm with far better potential turned those two months of unemployment from uncertain to a delightful sabbatical.

He learned to accept what was coming, good or bad. Alex had no problem learning to love that secret knowledge he gained while everyone around him, including the source of that knowledge, slept.

Disturbances in his own sleep, even combined with the hair-raising descriptions of starvation and war, were worth it to Alex in return for those glimpses of their future.

He felt almost like he had a secret relationship, one only he knew about, with whatever part of Etan had the dreams. Etan never seemed to remember them, no matter how badly he was upset by them in the moment.

Alex's guilt at keeping that secret combined uneasily with not having a clue how he would explain it.

Hey, did you know you predict the future in your sleep? Night after night, for years now? Probably shouldn't have kept that from you, huh?

The adventure faded when the dreams shifted not long after Alex turned twenty-five, Etan twenty-two.

The routine of sleeping and waking stayed the same, as did the open-eyed interaction with a man sound asleep. But the intensity and the frequency grew. Uneasy dreams nearly every night, and always about the same thing for weeks on end.

They had to go. They couldn't stay in Chicago. They had to go home.

Southeast.

Alex didn't have to look at a map to know what that meant.

He'd visited Etan's family in Virginia several times. The mountains and deep valleys fascinated him after a lifetime spent in the wide open Midwest, and Etan's parents were lovely. He felt more at home on his first visit than he ever had with his own family, who they saw far less often.

But those mountains scared him, too.

Alex felt like they traveled back in time, and not because they had to drive miles along twisty roads to find groceries or alcohol or much of anything else. He felt fundamentally out of place, never losing his awareness that he had no idea how to survive in such a place without Etan. He hadn't driven much since leaving the open, predictable grid of Wisconsin roads at seventeen.

Even if he'd fought the city traffic every single day for those eight years, he'd still be anxious about taking the wheel on the beautiful, unpredictable, and amazingly narrow roads around Wolf Branch.

Every time he was there, though, Alex never escaped the sense of alignment, of every leaf and creek and path through the wilderness pulling him deeper into whatever waited for him there.

Magic Alex didn't know the name for, awareness that seeped into his bones in the Virginia Highlands, turned up his senses and imagination to almost painful levels.

Much as Alex loved being in those mountains, among family who felt like his own, he didn't want to give up their life together in Chicago. The terror in Etan's strangely flat sleeping voice, and even worse, the tears in his unseeing eyes, broke through his resolution and his fear at last.

Chapter 5

Alex transformed everything he touched. He and Etan shared that same shoebox apartment overlooking Lake Michigan, but the space no longer felt oppressive. Alex's photos on the walls, his clothes in the wardrobe, his scent on the sheets turned the temporary shelter into a home both of them loved.

A home they both knew they had to leave before three years passed.

Alex walked into the living room with two glasses of bourbon and ice, their traditional sign it was time to put away work or study and spend the evening together after a challenging day. Etan closed the book he was pretending to study, hiding the page he'd been trying to read for the last half an hour. He normally managed to spend the time he needed and get it over with, but more than a strange lack of sleep kept him off balance lately.

His sense of things about to fly out of place had returned, more strongly than since he'd met Alex. He was terrified of what that was going to mean for both of them.

"Good stopping place?" Alex said.

He sat facing Etan on the dark grey couch, one of the upgrades he'd brought when he moved in. It fit under the broad windows overlooking the lake, by far the best feature in the cozy apartment, as if it had been custom built.

"As good as any. I'm not getting a damn thing done today."

"I'm not surprised, E. You're barely sleeping at all anymore."

"I'm sorry," Etan said, leaning over to kiss Alex on the cheek. "I didn't mean to keep you awake, too."

Alex stared out at the rough gray water of a storm coming in before speaking, leaving Etan's imagination to push him further into panic.

"No, that's not what's keeping me awake. It's what you say that does that. And the way I can't convince myself that every word isn't true."

Etan closed his eyes, not quite aware he was drawing his legs up against his belly. The goddamn dreams, the thing he'd been so scared of Alex or anyone else finding out about. Only his parents and grandparents had ever known about his nightmares.

Even he rarely remembered them besides waking up groggy and disoriented, suffering through the aftermath for the rest of the day.

"No, don't do that," Alex said. "Don't try to hide from me."

He moved the books and notebooks and gently pulled Etan toward him. Etan resisted for a second, then curled up with his head in his lover's lap.

"I never wanted you to know about the dreams. I feel crazy enough without you confirming it."

"Crazy isn't the question," Alex said, stroking Etan's hair. "Unless it's both of us. You missed me saying every word feels *true*."

"I don't even know what the dreams are, Alex. I know I have them, but I never remember a thing. That's not exactly stable."

"Well, have a drink and let me enlighten you."

Etan sat up, managing to keep himself from curling up into a knot of fear again. He drained the whiskey, watching Alex do the same.

"What you tell me in the middle of the night is all about how we can't stay here much longer. Something bad is going to happen, with the food supply I think, and none of the cities are going to be safe anymore. And we don't have much time to get ready before we're trapped along with everyone else who's not going to make it out."

Etan opened his mouth to argue, to protest, to at least keep Alex from saying another awful word. But the words had to be said, and he had to pay close attention. Every part of him knew understanding these dreams would be the difference between living and dying, for both of them and many others besides.

"Are you having the same dreams?" Etan said.

"Not at all. I normally sleep like a rock before and after you start talking. But this time, I'm too afraid to. They're not just words, E, not anymore. Don't you feel that?"

It was Etan's turn to stare out at the lake. The day had been cool and rainy, and the water was dark and choppy. He hadn't understood before Alex asked, but he felt exactly the same way and had for a few weeks now.

"Yeah. I've known something was wrong for a while. I didn't understand why."

"You said you never wanted me to know about the dreams," Alex said. He smiled and took Etan's hand. "I'm not sure why you thought I wouldn't notice, sleeping next to you every night, but it sounds like this isn't new. Does anyone else know about them?"

"My grandparents, Anne and Evan, the ones who grew up south of here. And my parents, a little. They tried to tell me I could talk to my cousins, but I never would let them tell me which ones. My grandmother had dreams that tended to come true, or at least they told me she did. A lot of them were nightmares when she was a kid."

"Maybe I don't understand, then. You keep saying we have to go home, over and over again. I don't think you mean Middle of Nowhere, Wisconsin, especially since you keep saying southeast. Does Virginia feel safer to you than Chicago even though your grandparents were from here?"

"Nowhere felt safe after they died, even after I moved up here," Etan said. "They were born a couple of hours south of the city, but my grandfather's family came from Virginia. That's why they moved back there in the end." He held his breath, then blurted out the rest before he could stop himself. "If we're going to talk about this like it could actually happen, the thing is anywhere out of a city seems like a better plan. Wisconsin is too open, at least where you're from. Nowhere good to hide."

Alex only nodded.

"Can't disagree with you there. I felt that way for seventeen years in Fond du Lac. Now tell me what we'll be hiding from, E. What's going to send us running southeast when both of us love it right here in Chicago? Can you remember?"

The dream opened in Etan's mind as if Alex's words, his attention, slowly turned on the lights on a darkened stage.

A stage the size of the whole world, the play too harrowing for anyone to sit through.

"You said I talk about the food supply, right?" Etan waited for Alex to nod. "I keep thinking about the way my family in Virginia kept food stored, especially for the winter, even with grocery stores in town. An old-school pantry and cellar aren't going to be enough for whatever this thing is. The air, the water, even the soil. It's all poison. Things won't grow properly anymore. Masses of people trapped in cities, and I know hardly any of them are going to make it."

Etan gasped, shocked and relieved that he'd said so much. He hadn't talked about anything he'd dreamed since his grandparents died when he was sixteen. Old enough to realize knowing he had nightmares but being unable to remember them was exactly the kind of strange he wanted to keep to himself.

"Did you remember any of that before I asked you?" Alex said. He was holding both of Etan's hands now, the contact like a lifeline in that choppy lake.

"Only the part about storing food. I don't really remember details of the rest. It's just... It feels true. Now you tell me something."

"You're wondering why I would believe you?"

Etan couldn't help returning Alex's smile. The tension pulling all of his nerves and muscles to the breaking point eased up enough for him to breathe.

"Most people wouldn't," Etan said. "Most people would have

already been on the phone to the psych ward. That's another thing about my grandmother. She spent time there more than once when she was young. She remembered all of her dreams, though."

"*Most people* don't know you as well as I do. From what you tell me, no one has slept beside you for more than a night, either. What I've been hiding from you is how the things you mutter in the night have a strong tendency to come true. If I could get you to dream about the stock market or sports, we'd never have to worry about money again."

"Bullshit," Etan said, unable to hide the flush spreading across his face. His whole body felt like he was trapped in the white hot spotlight on that vast stage. "You're making this up."

"I can't think of one damn reason why I'd make something like this up. Even I'm not enough of a jerk to think that would be funny. But let's see."

Alex took a deep breath and leaned closer, tilting his head and staring into Etan's eyes.

"Ever wonder why I'm never surprised by an odd phone call? How I knew exactly when I'd get laid off, and when I'd get this job? Why I already have my time off arranged anytime we have to go to a funeral or wedding or whatever else comes up? People probably think I'm the one who can predict the future."

"You can fucking have it, then, Alex!" Etan pulled his hands away and sat back. "I've hated this since it started, even more once I knew it drove my grandmother half crazy. If I could make it stop right this second I would!"

Alex smiled a tiny bit.

"You've always said you knew you'd meet me that night, at that stupid college hook up party in the middle of the biggest blizzard in twenty years. Wish you'd stayed home instead of going home with me that night?"

"Not usually," Etan said, trying to catch his breath. "Right now, maybe."

What an asshole he was, shouting like that. Alex had no way to know how desperately Etan needed to keep the damn nightmares a secret. How terrified he was of having as much trouble as his grandmother did. Etan hadn't exactly been honest about any of it.

"Good thing you didn't know any better." Alex brushed the back of his fingers along Etan's cheek. "You've never told me how you knew. Did you dream about that night before it happened? About me?"

"I don't know. Maybe. Probably. I hate talking about this, Alex."

"Well, if even half of what I've been hearing and feeling is true, we're both going to have to be a hell of a lot more honest. It's way too late for me, sweetie. I'm not going anywhere. Is the way you know things more than dreams?"

Chapter 6

Etan forced his breathing to slow, hoping his heart would follow. He kept seeing his grandmother's green eyes, same as his and his father's. Near the end, he didn't think she knew who she was talking to, but she seemed driven, compelled to get the words out. Words that hadn't made sense to him then, but Etan, his father, and especially his grandfather listened to every one. That might be the key to everything now.

Maybe talking to the man he trusted more than anyone else would keep this thing from eating him alive like it tried to devour her.

"That night, lots of times, I can feel something moving toward me," Etan said, speaking slowly. "Once in a while I see an image, but usually I get the sense of a piece moving into place. I knew a big change was coming that night, and I knew it would be good. It has been."

Now Alex looked away and blushed, but not before Etan saw his smile. He wished they could continue along this path, warm and safe with the storm outside the window. Go back to that first night and discover each other's bodies, minds, and hearts all over again.

But what he felt shifting into alignment now, blasting everything else out of place, was too huge and moving too fast to ignore.

"What I feel now is just as big, maybe bigger," he said. "And nothing will ever be the same again. When you asked me about it, my mind focused, I think. Or cleared. Whatever's coming is going to break everything."

Alex groaned, soft and low, but Etan heard it. He nodded, his blue eyes terrified.

"That's what I've been feeling, Etan. Everything's going to break. Your dreams are part of it, but this comes from inside me, too."

Alex looked down, at the fist he'd made so tightly the tendons stood out along his wrist.

"What comes from you, Alex? What's got you that upset?"

"You said you had your grandmother to talk to about all of this. I haven't had anyone. I've never mentioned a word of this to a single person. And I'm the one who said we had to be more honest with each other."

He opened his fist, staring at the red half circles in his palm. Etan rubbed his hand.

"I didn't know I was going to meet you that night," he said, looking at Etan. "But I did know something was going to happen. I don't have dreams like you do, or visions or anything like that. It's not that easy to explain."

"You think this is easy?" Etan struggled not to laugh with Alex so anxious. "You missed your chance to turn me in to the shadowy authorities for having dreams that predict the future. You're stuck with me now."

"I see..." Alex stared at the lake again, opening and closing his mouth. "Patterns is the clearest way to put it. Movement and alignment all around me when something's going to happen. Before I left Fond du Lac, everything I saw for months lined up and pointed toward Chicago. Clouds, leaves blowing down the street, ripples in water. All I had to do was follow whatever was pulling me. The rest was effortless."

"What about the night you met me?"

"Nothing until I was outside the apartment, not really. Then the light and the snow and the people inside pointed me to you. I couldn't even see anyone else's face in the room, E. Only yours."

His own internal world whirled and adjusted, lining up with the forces inside and around Alex. Completing the synchronization that started the second he'd seen Alex walk through the door and into his life.

"You did walk right toward me."

"Thank the gods," Alex said, his tense face relaxing into a small smile. He brought Etan's hand to his lips, then held both of his hands again. "I never thought I would admit this, not even to you, but whatever these dreams are feels even bigger to me, too. I see the same patterns I did before, pointing in the same direction. Southeast."

"But it doesn't make any sense," Etan said, pulling one hand away to rub his eyes. "It's probably stress over these damn classes and worrying about whether I should keep going or give it up and get a job. I *am* studying fucking environmental policy right now, every-thing that can go wrong."

"That's something else you forget. I've already been out in the world for a few years instead of neck deep in academia. Some strange things are starting to happen. I might not have thought much about it besides typical gloom and doom bullshit, but it's close enough to make me uncomfortable."

"What things?" Etan whispered.

He would have sworn the surface of his brain was swelling, bubbling up, trying to change shape. Alex's words, and his belief in these crazy dreams, set off a change neither of them would be able to stop.

"Remember the bees and other pollinators having trouble a while back? When a bunch of them died off, before we were born? Stories about that happening again are springing up all over the world. Faster than back then when it started, too, and no one knows why. Everyone just figured we had it beat, so all these years later we're as dependent on them for our food as ever."

Etan rubbed his arms, trying to stop the crawling sensation before it could spread to his whole body. He'd refused to visit his grandfather Evan's bee hives with all the other kids, no matter how much they picked on him about being scared. Yet another thing he had in common with his grandmother.

She'd told him she never liked bees, either. In fact…

"Alex. My grandmother told me she dreamed about bees, all the time when she was a teenager. Awful dreams. Gods, she told me she saw all of the bees dying, then almost all the people dying not long after."

Etan realized he was shivering when Alex moved closer and put both arms around him. He grasped his lover's strong forearms and tried to keep his teeth from chattering.

"She told you that? How old were you?"

"This was not long before she passed, so I was fourteen, fifteen. Their house wasn't far from us, so I was over there all the time. I guess I was old enough, but by then she was getting a lot more honest than she should have been."

"You were just a *baby*." The harsh edge in his voice surprised Etan. "If it upsets you like this now, she definitely shouldn't have told you when you were so young."

"No, listen. Dad told me she wanted to make sure we were all ready just in case we had the dreams too. It was the right thing, Alex. Gemaw said that was what made it so bad for her, when no one believed her and she had to hide what was going on."

"Gemaw?" Alex said. "That's a new one on me, sweetie."

The laughter, always sweeter when they shared it, stopped most of the trembling.

"Welcome to the Griffith family, sugar pie. Just wait till we figure out what to call you when the time comes."

"That's something else we haven't talked about as much as we should have if any of this is going to happen," Alex said. "Maybe we should go ahead and get the DNA merge now instead of when we're ready to have kids. Hang on, hear me out."

Etan hadn't realized he was shaking his head.

"If everything's going to go to hell, this is the last thing we should be worrying about. If things get bad enough, we'll barely be able to keep ourselves alive, much less kids."

"No, listen, you stubborn jackass," Alex said. "We get it done while we can, then all we're worried about is keeping the cells frozen."

"What, in a cooler? And we're still talking about raising children at the end of the world."

Alex sighed, rolling his eyes at the same time. Etan knew that combination well, but he knew he was right no matter how upset Alex was.

"Tell me all of it, then," Alex said. "You feel like food supply is going to be a problem. That feels right to me. Stores barely have a few days' worth at the best of times with the way distribution works. What about technology? What about the power grid? All the solar panels and windmills in the world, all over the Midwest and Southwest—and in your Blue Ridge Mountains, I might add—won't do a damn bit of good if transmission fails, will they?"

"I don't feel like much of anything is going to do a damn bit of good. What if this is what my grandmother dreamed about, Alex? She told me hardly anyone survives anywhere in the world."

Alex scowled, his pale eyebrows drawing together. His ability to hold on to his natural optimism no matter how gloomy Etan got was normally one of the best things about the two of them. Right now it was pissing Etan off.

"But she didn't say *no one* survived. Maybe your dreams and hers mean someone will."

"We can't argue about this right now," Etan said, closing his eyes and tilting his head from side to side. His neck muscles felt like over-coiled springs. "If you're telling me you believe this, that the whole fucking world is going to fall apart, we have bigger things to deal with. Right?"

Alex stared at Etan for a few seconds, then shrugged and shook his head at the same time. Yes, he was letting the discussion about having children go for now. And yes, it would come back up again.

"Just promise me you'll tell me if you feel differently? About the food thing, I mean. I don't want to leave here any more than you do, but my gut is telling me we don't have a hell of a lot of choice. Or we won't before long."

"I promise," Etan said. "You'll be the first to know, since I don't even remember the blasted dreams. But I promise."

Alex smiled, but it barely touched his eyes. He gazed out at the lake again for a long time. His breathing slowed, and his grip on Etan's hand slowly tightened. When he finally turned back, tears stood in his eyelashes.

"What are we going to do, E?" Alex whispered. His optimism and confidence vanished in the slightest downward movement of his head, the slump of his shoulders. "How are we going to get through this?"

Chapter 7

THE BUSY OFFICE hummed around Alex, his co-workers going about their days, and their lives, as if everything were perfectly normal. Floor to ceiling windows dimmed strategically with the sun to maximize heat gain or loss as well as showcase the stunning views of downtown Chicago along the corridor wall. Everyone buzzed with excitement over news of the major renewable energy contract their small firm had just been awarded.

Alex's door was usually open, the blinds on his window raised, when he was there. He enjoyed the white noise and talking with other engineers and managers about their various projects.

Today he had the door closed and the shade drawn. The only light in his office came from his monitor.

The email was one he'd been struggling for, hoping for, daydreaming about for months. Long hours of work and planning, and the most careful and well thought out proposal he'd ever put together, were a huge part of the success the whole firm was celebrating today.

That approval notice arrived with an offer of Alex serving as the project manager. Success at such a huge role would bring promotion not far behind, and eventually a partnership.

For once, he wished he'd at least had the chance to be surprised. He'd known what was coming for the last several nights.

Instead of joining in the elation all around him, Alex was barely managing not to puke all over himself.

None of that was going to happen. Not only because of Etan's strange and insistent dreams about the end of the world, though that was a factor.

Alex was about to quit the perfect job for him, better than he'd imagined for himself or anyone else, on the day of his biggest success.

He rubbed at his mouth, the scratchy noise of his short beard clear in the silence. Etan's idea of just not showing up for work any more had its appeal, especially now that he was faced with walking into his manager's office and going through with this. The temptation to simply disappear threatened to take over Alex's mind and body, more and more the longer he sat there staring at the email.

He knew he'd never do such a thing. Not only because it was the coward's way out, a choice he'd never made in his life and didn't intend to start now. The real reason was hard to admit to himself. He doubted he'd ever admit it to Etan.

Deep in his mind, so deep he could barely hear the nervous whisper, Alex wasn't completely sure the dreams meant anything. Not on this scale, so much bigger than predicting a phone call or wedding or funeral.

Alex was willing to go with his lover on this terrifying journey into a new life. He wasn't willing to burn any more bridges than he had to on the way out of town.

If this turned out to be a tremendous mistake, some kind of misunderstanding or flat out nonsense, begging to get his job back would be distasteful to him in the extreme. Even hard core groveling likely wouldn't work after Alex let everyone down in such a spectacular fashion on the biggest day in the firm's history, one he'd played a huge role in bringing to reality.

But disappearing without a word would make his return here or to any other firm in Chicago impossible.

If only the damn dreams had started sooner. Then he could

have…what, exactly? Quit sooner, with even less to go on and less money to go with? Slack off at the job he loved so much instead of working harder than he ever had in his life? Manage to fuck something else up badly enough that he'd get fired before he had to quit?

No matter how difficult the next half hour turned out to be, Alex didn't have any of those options in him. At least walking in there and facing this like a man—a terribly reluctant and anxious man who was still determined to do the right thing—would be true to who he was in his heart.

His phone buzzed in his pocket, and he didn't have to look to know who was calling. Turning his life on end was about to get a hell of a lot more difficult. Alex saw exactly the name he expected to when he glanced at the screen.

May as well get all the suck over with for one day and move on.

"Hi Mom."

"Hi Alex. Do you have a minute?"

"Sure. I've got all the time in the world."

She laughed, and Alex wished he could laugh with her.

"You're every bit as much a workaholic as I am, son. You might have surpassed me over the past few months."

"You're right about that," Alex said, leaning back in his chair and closing his eyes. "What's up?"

"I'm getting the plans together for your father's birthday party next month. Will you be able to get that Friday off, or do we need to wait until Saturday?"

Alex was usually grateful for his mother's obsessive planning for his father's birthday, for some reason far more important to her than any other national holiday. Including her own birthday, or any of her children's. That gave him the out of keeping visits down to a once a year minimum most of the time.

This time, he doubted he'd make it up to Fond du Lac at all this year. And if Etan's dreams held true like they had for the last three years, like his grandmother Anne's had, Alex had already made his last visit.

"I doubt we're going to be able to make it." He tapped the back of the phone, disgusted with his own weak language. "No, I meant to say we're not going to make it. I'm sorry."

The silence stretched out long enough for Alex to slowly count to ten.

"I'm sure you can explain to your manager that you need at least one day off," she finally said. "You can fly up on Saturday morning and fly back that night. Even I don't work the *whole* weekend. Not that often, anyway."

"It's not for work, Mom. That's not going to be a problem much longer."

"Not a problem? I don't like the way your voice sounds, Alex. Maybe you better tell me what's going on."

The pause was on Alex's side this time. He didn't like the way her voice sounded, either. And there wasn't a damn thing he could do about that. He couldn't disappear from his parents' lives with no explanation any more than he could from his job.

He couldn't even manage the lie they were going to tell Etan's family about his getting laid off again. His mother would quite possibly investigate that story. He knew she'd done that with his first job. Looking for investment opportunities, so she'd said.

Alex knew better.

"I'm resigning today." He took a deep breath. "And we're moving."

"Resigning. You're obviously moving for a better position, then. Why don't you tell me about that?"

"There's nothing to tell. We're moving to Virginia where Etan's family is. We'll worry about jobs when we get down there."

"*Jobs?* You have worked long and hard to have a career, young man, and a damn good one, not so you can settle for whatever manual labor you scratch up out of the dirt. Unless there's some secret enclave of engineering hidden away in the backwoods, I have to be missing something. What the hell is going on, Alex?"

He rubbed his mouth again, blowing through his fingers. This conversation was going about as well as he expected.

"You're not missing anything, except understanding that I've been out here making decisions for myself for almost ten years now. We both need a change, and we're making one. That's all."

"So first you support him so he can keep going to school, and now he's got you leaving your whole life behind to disappear into the middle of nowhere. I know you love him, son, but don't you think this has gone far enough? Etan might not understand what you've been working so hard for."

"Just stop, Mom. That's enough." Alex dug the heel of his hand into his thigh, over and over again. "Etan understands more than you know, and he knows exactly how hard this is for me. He's giving up a lot, too.

"Giving up what? A free ride on your coattails, except now that's a free ride into poverty. Right back where he came from."

"Well, it's been great talking to you," Alex said through his teeth. "I'll let you know when we get settled. Take care."

"Don't you dare-"

Alex ended the call, then turned the phone off. He glanced back at the email, snorting at how upset he'd been before his mother called. At least talking to his manager would be a hell of a lot easier now.

Talking to his father once his mother shared her big news would be far worse, if he even bothered after that disaster.

He gasped when he stood, the long muscles of his right thigh cramping. He'd at least have a bruise to deal with, if not spend the next few days limping while they got most of their belongings ready to sell and packed up what was left.

Something to remember his family by.

Chapter 8

WHEN THEY LEFT Chicago for what they both knew to be the last time, Etan didn't miss how Alex grew more quiet as the terrain changed. Farmland and orderly rows and divisions fell to wild, disorganized trees, rocks, and streams. The flat, uncurving highway they'd followed for hundreds of miles—along with ruler-straight roads jutting off at regular intervals—flowed into curving roads with the mountains of eastern Kentucky soaring high alongside.

After hours of Illinois and then Indiana, Etan had to admit not being able to see more than a few hundred yards ahead was shocking. The green even changed, from the pale cultivated version of hundreds of acres of corn and soybeans dotted with bright wind turbines to the wild hues of fir, oaks, maples, and more other trees and brush than he knew the names for.

The pace slowed a bit as well, with some cars flying through on the way further south, especially when they exited the main artery of I-64 for Mountain Parkway. The smaller road that followed cut through deep valleys alongside a massive lake for this part of the country, with equally massive antiquated coal power plants scarring the land.

Even the arrangements of those towering white wind turbines

that helped replace those power plants changed as they continued southeast. The orderly grids of Illinois and Indiana, massive curving blades all spinning at the same height, gave way to undulating waves that followed the ridgelines. Alex never failed to comment on how they seemed to rise up out of the earth, showing contours of the land they couldn't see any other way.

Instead of sharing one of what seemed like a thousand stories of a summer spent helping build several turbines in Indiana, he didn't say a word about that or anything else.

Alex watched the traffic, sometimes pretending to pay attention to the navigation computer Etan didn't need. They weren't in his sleek autonav sedan, the one Alex had been so thrilled to buy for Etan when he'd gotten his second job out of college.

The job he'd fought for, the one he'd worked so hard to get qualified for and excelled in.

The one he'd quit a few days before.

Etan now drove an antique, a hybrid van with options for gas, electric, and manual navigation. He'd forced himself to shut down the primitive autonav at their last stop, reasoning he should have at least a little bit of practice with handling the car himself. He hadn't done such a thing since his driver training years ago. Many of these cars were still on the road for stubborn drivers, those who were convinced they could do better than any computer no matter how qualified and tested.

Etan didn't feel that way, not even a little bit. Having to watch the other cars, his speed, and the steep curves all at the same time left him anxious and exhausted. He had plenty of relatives who did feel they were superior to even the newest network-controlled vehicles.

He'd refused to ride with them once he was old enough to understand what they were standing up for. The right to be as erratic and unpredictable as they wanted. And he understood as he got older that he'd been getting a sense of how some of them would end up.

He'd missed being in more than one wreck not long before it happened.

This van, reasonably well-maintained and easy enough to drive, just made more sense with the disaster both of them sensed growing closer every day. Once the grid failed, and the technology that controlled so many of the cars around them with it, being able to move around under their own power would be a tremendous advantage.

At least until the gas ran out. And he was afraid depending on the grid to charge an electric vehicle would quickly turn the most modern cars into junk.

As Etan navigated the long, sweeping curve off the parkway, trying not to get too nervous maneuvering through the choked streets of a tiny historic town, he knew he had to get Alex talking. Confirming his suspicions about what the problem was, or at least having Alex admit it, wouldn't be pleasant no matter what.

Going through that with Etan's very close and very curious family right there would make everything a thousand times worse. He didn't need any kind of prescience or dreams to know that.

"Need to stop for anything?" he said, glancing at Alex.

"I'm fine. We're not even an hour away, right?"

"Just over an hour, sweetie."

Alex had made the trip several times over the past three years, but usually for some kind of happy occasion. A couple of funerals, of course, but generally it was for a wedding or a holiday. He seemed to enjoy the mountains once he got used to being in such a different landscape.

"I know this is hard for you," Etan said, trying to feel his way forward. The only sense he got was Alex had to say something. "Can I do anything to help?"

"I doubt it. I'm not exactly coming to my new life in triumph, am I?"

"I don't know what else we could have done. We can still change our story if we need to, but we couldn't stay in the city."

Alex breathed deeply, then let it out in a harsh rush.

"Yeah, I know. I understand. I'm not arguing about that. We have to move, I get it. I'm not thrilled about telling everyone I lost my job. Again."

"It was your idea to-"

"I know it was my idea!" Alex winced, looking at Etan. "I'm sorry. I loved that job, you know? It was exactly what all those years of busting my ass in school were for. I feel like such a fucking bum, moving down here to sponge off your family."

"You know this is only for a little while, right? I doubt we have a year left."

"Probably not even a year from the way I feel. And the way you've been dreaming. I just don't love having to look your parents in the eye when they think I couldn't keep a damn job for more than a couple of years. I was supposed to be the one keeping us going while you finished up school, remember?"

Etan concentrated on the road, letting his lover get through his frustration. This was all a horrible game, a series of lies neither one of them wanted to tell. A game they were both sure they had to play well to give anyone a chance to survive.

"You *would* have kept us going, Alex, and a hell of a lot more. We both know that. I don't want to imagine how hard it is to give up your career. I never even got there. I'll be lying to them too. I have no intention of working on a thesis about environmental risk management. It wouldn't do any good if I did. The environment is pretty much screwed already, and no one will be alive to review the damn thing."

Alex snorted, turning to Etan and taking his hand. The tension was slowly leaving the car.

"At least your lie is one you could have been proud of if it were true. You would have been trying to accomplish something. Pathetic as it sounds, my pride is taking a beating even though I know this will all be over before another year passes."

"You'll be in the pressure cooker, I'm afraid. People I went to high school with have been waiting for me to fail and run back here with my tail between my legs since the day I left. Well, some of them have. My parents will be fine, Alex. They both love you. But the others, just ignore their hillbilly asses. They're not worth worrying about even if you wanted to."

The narrow streets full of pedestrians slowly opened up to a clearer road, nowhere near as easy to navigate as the interstate. Etan loved the way the road seemed to sink down into the mountains, as if he were being welcomed home by the land around them.

No matter how much he loved Chicago and everything the city had to offer him, a deep part of him relaxed and uncoiled the further he moved into the land of his birth.

"Want to drive for a while?" he said. He knew the answer very well.

"Are you crazy? I'd somehow manage to run us into the side of a mountain even with the autonav. If I try driving this thing, we won't make it a hundred feet."

"You may have to get used to it, you know. What if we both have to drive? Or what if I can't for some reason? You can't hide behind being a spoiled non-driving city boy forever down here."

Etan tried to keep a straight face until Alex caught up with him. The lingering upset and stress showed when it took Alex several seconds longer than his normal instantaneous understanding of Etan's humor.

"Well, I guess we'll have to walk, then. Or find donkeys or mules or something. You still have those down here, right?"

"Absolutely. Along with the outhouses and swimming holes down in the creek. That's how I got ready for school every morning."

The van chugged a bit going up a long hill, forcing Etan into a far less humorous mood.

"Alex, have you thought about that? What if we do end up using goddamn holes in the ground? I'm lying through my teeth about a thesis, but I know enough about water chemistry to know we don't have any good way to keep the water clean. Not that they do in the cities."

"We'll be a hell of a lot better off here than there from what you've been seeing lately," Alex said, the lightness missing from his own voice as well. "Whatever we can do here will be safer than all the water that can be poisoned at once in a city reservoir. Listen, this is going to sound like a joke but it isn't. Are there still survivalists down here? I think there still are in Missouri, in the Ozarks."

"What, like the militia types?" Etan took his eyes off the road at a stoplight before their last turn. Alex looked completely serious. "I guess there probably are. I'm sure I'm related to some of them. I don't know a whole lot about it. I was in too big a hurry to get out of here."

"We may want to see what we can learn," Alex said. "I read a bunch of books about that stuff, back when I wanted to get away from Wisconsin and everywhere else in the world sounded like a better option. These people were determined the old government was coming to take away their food or their guns or something. They stockpiled canned goods, water, weapons, all of it. They had to have some way to purify water and deal with waste and such."

"I'm sure I have a cousin or two with those same books. Maybe the original copies. We'll probably have great luck with my Grandpa Evan's books. He was a fiend for that kind of stuff. He was collecting them back when those people were still everywhere. He has a private library in the house we're going to be living in."

"Didn't your grandmother say something about a library?" Alex smiled. "Your Gemaw?"

"Yeah, smart ass, she did." Etan was silent for a few seconds, following a steep curve and trying to think of how to put it. "She told me she dreamed about a giant library, the really awful dreams. She was trapped in there watching a bunch of giant screens. The floors, the walls, the ceilings, everything was a screen showing how people were going to die in great detail. She couldn't make it stop and she couldn't get away."

"How old was she then?"

"She was eleven or twelve, same as when I started having the dreams. But she remembered all of them most of the time. That drove her kind of crazy, I think. Before she figured out some way to keep them under control."

"That's horrible. No wonder she wanted to warn you. I know you hate to talk about it, but I've been wondering if your dreams are going to get worse as this thing gets closer. They have been over the past year or so."

"Worried you'll have to get me put away after all?" Etan said. He wasn't quite joking.

"Not a bit. I've been feeling it more lately. Seeing it all around us. I was hoping I could do something to help. Keep you calmer or whatever. Don't be such an asshole."

"I'm sorry. It still makes me nervous to talk about the dreams. I always thought I was going crazy, unless I was with my grandparents. Or with you. What she told me was she talked to my grandfather about the dreams. Once she did that, she started to feel calmer."

"Did hers ever stop?"

"No, I don't think they stopped until she died. But talking to him made all the difference. That and she said something about other things moving into place. That I do understand. I felt that way when I met you."

"Do you feel that way about moving here, E? About making such a big change?"

Etan wished he could say yes, that he felt everything in its right place. A bit of the tension did seem to be shifting, changing, but it wasn't going away. Different direction or not, the velocity, the sense of calamity heading toward them, was stronger with every mile he drove.

"I feel like I can stop worrying so much about getting us out of the city," he said. "Now I can worry a little bit more about getting us through the next couple of years. I'm not sure if that's better or worse. What does it feel like to you?"

Alex looked around at the narrowing road twisting through a deep green and blue valley, following the path of a river like so many of the roads here did. They were in shadow hours before the sun set.

"Right now I feel the same way I always do when we first get here. I can't see far enough. I have no idea what's coming around the next corner. Anything in the world could be waiting for us, and I can't do a thing to stop it. I'm scared to death I'm going to let us both down."

Etan closed his eyes for a second, his heart turning into a ball of hot water in his throat. That aspect of being the younger one, still a kid in school, of feeling like Alex was sometimes the mature adult between the two of them, was usually more annoying than anything.

Right now he felt like he was failing the person he cared more about than anyone else.

"I don't know if this helps or not," he said. "But I'm the one who should be figuring this kind of stuff out now that we're down here. I'm supposed to know my way around, or at least I should. I'm the native, right? Trust me, Alex. I don't like this role reversal thing any more than you do."

Etan slowed, remembering to put his turn signal on at the last second. One left turn, a quick drive of a few miles past this very small town, and they'd be face to face with the dramatic, sudden change in their lives.

Nowhere left to hide.

Barely a month ago, they'd been happy in Chicago, moving forward with their lives. Looking forward to Etan finishing school, Alex getting promoted again. Buying their own place, putting down roots. Starting the family that was now eternally delayed.

Today they were both jobless and homeless, everything they'd worked for and planned and dreamed of derailed. Their lives on permanent hold. And they had to make believe all of this was according to a bigger plan, one they'd had any part in creating.

Alex either read Etan's mind, or his own mind was putting him through worse. He spoke as they took the last turn, his voice weak and airy.

"I think I'm going to be sick."

Etan glanced over, and Alex was indeed pale and sweaty. A sprinkling of freckles across his cheeks and nose stood out more than they usually did unless he was ill. He'd gotten carsick on their first couple of trips a few years ago. Etan didn't believe the change in elevation and terrain were creating the trouble now.

"Let me pull over. We'll walk around for a little while. Get you something to drink."

"If we stop now, I'm never going to make it," Alex said. "Maybe your family and everyone else will have mercy on me if they remember I'm the new kid."

"Don't worry. They won't forget that anytime soon. Won't be

long until none of that matters anymore. Sure you don't need to stop?"

"It's just hitting me all at once. We're never going to leave here, are we? This is it, live or die. This is it."

Chapter 9

Etan was in for his own surprise when he parked in front of his grandparents' house. His heart pounded, his gut twisted. As was often the case, Alex recovered by having someone to help. He leaned over and touched the back of Etan's neck

"You okay?"

"I haven't been here since they died." Etan rubbed his face, not surprised by the clammy sweat there.

He and Alex were only half a mile past his parents' house, but they seemed to be miles from another human being. From this small valley set back from the road, the only thing anyone could see was mountains covered in thick trees. The house was brick, one-story, with a few steps leading to the broad screened-in porch. A dark brown steel roof helped the house blend into the tree line.

Everything looked exactly the same, and that somehow made it a thousand times worse. His grandparents' blue sedan was still sitting in the driveway, the same gas-powered model they'd driven south from Illinois decades ago. All the same trees, the brightly painted wooden lawn furniture, the flowers his grandmother planted and cared for so carefully.

It wouldn't have surprised Etan to see both of them opening the door, arms around each other's waists, smiling and so happy to see him.

Instead of the huge group of people Etan and certainly Alex had been afraid of, the place was deserted. He couldn't hear anything but their footsteps through the grass and the breeze blowing through the swaying oaks and pines.

"Do you have a key?" Alex said. He looked much better now that he was out of the car and moving around.

"No. I expected someone to be here."

They walked toward the porch, Etan hoping no one had moved the hiding place in the last several years. He found the stone sculpture of two stylized adults with a child: a gift from Etan's grandparents who'd lived their whole lives in Illinois. He tilted it back to reveal two keys on a small metal ring.

"See," he said, grinning at Alex, trying to reassure himself. "Nothing ever changes here."

Inside the house was just as disorienting. All the low, comfortable furniture covered in dark greens and browns was unchanged, as were the pictures of family and locations from all over the world on the tan walls. The arched passage, so like the ones in their apartment back in Chicago, revealed the next small room where his grandfather's books still lined every inch of space.

Alex picked up a small blue envelope from the table beside the door. *Welcome Home* was written in Etan's mother's looping script.

"Go ahead," Etan said. "This place is way too small for us to have secrets."

"The house or the town?"

Alex winked as he opened the envelope. He smiled as he read, and a couple of tears spilled over before he could catch them. He handed the note to Etan, then stood close with his hand on his lower back.

So glad our beautiful young men are home! Get some rest, get settled in. Stocked up a little, wasn't sure what you wanted. Tried to get your favorites, but don't know Alex's yet! Give us a call when you're ready for company.

Love, Mom and Dad.

"My favorites?" Alex said.

"Unless my mother has changed drastically, there'll be more food in the kitchen than we ever had our apartment. Come on. You hungry?"

"More curious than hungry," Alex said. He followed Etan through the library toward the kitchen. "Looks like we have all the research materials we'll ever need."

All four walls were covered floor-to-ceiling with bookshelves stuffed full of every sort of book Etan could imagine. He flinched again when he saw the two old fashioned burgundy wingback chairs sitting by the window, a huge matching ottoman positioned for both of them. His grandmother's fluffy pink blanket was still folded up on hers.

He'd spent many happy evenings curled up under that blanket with her until he got too big to fit in the chair.

"Wait till you see their computers," he said. "They may be a little bit outdated, but we'll never get to the end of everything stored there. No cellular to speak of in this little valley, and only satellite TV for as long as that lasts. All the peace and quiet either of us can stand."

The kitchen was small, only a few paces across, but with everything painted a bright, cheery yellow, it was more welcoming than the dark, modern space they'd left behind.

True to her word, Etan's mother had filled the refrigerator and all the cabinets. A plate full of chocolate chip cookies sat beside a bottle of their favorite bourbon on the counter, everything wrapped in red ribbon. Two shot glasses engraved with the same roses as the bottle stood in front.

"She did pretty well with my favorites," Alex said. "Maybe I *am* gonna like it here."

Chapter 10

A couple of shots of their welcome gift, combined with relief of being off the road, led to Alex and Etan's best lovemaking in a long while. That feeling of being in the eye of the storm, in a calm they both knew they'd miss when it was over, heightened every touch, taste, smell, even with bodies long familiar.

Difficult times were ahead, neither of them doubted that. But they'd gotten through a huge part of their journey with hard-earned time for recovery.

As often happened after they had sex, Etan's plans for unloading everything right away dissolved when he fell deeply asleep. Alex didn't hesitate to take advantage of time on his own, wide awake, to prowl around their new home.

Just as predictably, he went straight to the library at the heart of the small house.

The space wasn't large, only a few of Alex's long strides across in any direction. Anne and Evan had managed to pack a remarkable number of books into every available inch, with dark stained wooden shelves reaching almost to the low ceiling and across the doorways and windows. They ranged from tall and deep at the bottom, with room enough for textbooks and large format photo books, to two rows perfectly fitted for small paperbacks all around the top.

Alex walked slowly around the shelves, his eyes drinking in the remarkable variety, his fingers brushing smooth or slick or scratchy spines.

He'd never seen so many physical books in one house. All of his textbooks in high school and most in college had been electronic, and Alex himself only owned a few printed reference books.

After his first circuit, Alex stood in the middle of the room, turning as he examined the photographs on the top shelf. In three years of hearing about Etan's grandparents, he only had a vague idea of what they looked like. Now that he could see pictures of her, he suspected he would have recognized Anne in a crowd of strangers.

Etan was an eerily perfect male version of her, from his green eyes to his light brown hair to his fine, almost delicate features.

Etan's grandfather Evan had the most striking blue eyes Alex had ever seen, pale but not cold at all. His smile was far too gentle and warm for that. The photos of the three of them, so clearly delighted to be together, lifted a bit of the discomfort and sadness from Alex's heart.

The books ignited his curiosity, and not just because he'd never had the chance to get his hands on so much paper. The arrangements of the shapes and colors of those hundreds of spines shaped an unmistakable pattern, one that cried out to his restless mind.

Logic and reason told him that spark, that need to dig into everything laid out before him like a road map, was only a coincidence. But he knew better, from Etan's stories of his grandparents, and from his dreams.

Evan surely grew up every bit as ignorant of dreams and their potential as Alex had. Yet Evan had been the witness to Anne's dreams, the one who listened and understood and did his best to give comfort in the middle of the night.

Alex wouldn't have been surprised if Evan knew exactly what he was doing when he arranged these shelves. He'd be more surprised if Etan's grandfather had *not* left a vital secret message somewhere in all these shelves.

A message especially, and only, for Alex's eyes.

He glanced around the room again, eyes unfocused, mind at last calm and ready. The colors and shapes resolved to a point. A beginning.

Alex pulled a book off the highest shelf, settled himself in the larger of the two chairs, and started to read.

Chapter 11

A few hours later, Etan and Alex walked down to the house Etan grew up in. Dinner with only the four of them felt like the perfect way for Alex to get comfortable without getting overwhelmed. A bit of Alex's unusual gloom seemed to have lifted with a solid bit of sleep. But Etan suspected Alex wouldn't quite be back to his normal, cheerful self just yet.

The younger Griffith's house was almost as private as Etan's grandparents' retirement home, two stories and white wooden siding hidden from the main road by trees and a curving gravel driveway. More yard hid behind the house rather than stretching out in front like at Evan and Anne's house. And unlike what seemed like a museum down the road, this one changed constantly.

Furniture shifted inside and out, along with paint colors, carpet, and an endless variety of projects. Etan rarely needed his decorating and repair skills once he'd taken up apartment living, but he had a feeling he'd soon be thankful to have them.

They smelled steaks on the grill before they could even see the house.

"Ready for this?" Etan said, taking Alex's hand.

"I have been here before. I don't think I've grown a third arm or anything since last time."

"You've never been guest of honor at a welcome home sympathy dinner before. My parents and all my other relatives are of the firm opinion that just about anything can be made better with a good enough meal. I'll have to roll you back up the mountain tonight."

They rounded the last curve to see the main feature of the small front yard had been upgraded yet again. The massive brick grill, complete with three cooking areas, including one for old-fashioned charcoal to complement the gas, had gained an miniature roof against hot sun or rainy weather. The stone and brick patio a few feet away now held low lounge chairs with thick cushions beside a long picnic table.

Etan's father stood with his back to them, moving with athletic grace between the three surfaces. Connor Griffith alternated whistling and singing to himself, and Etan didn't need to see his dad's face to know he was smiling.

Etan's mother stepped out onto the screened-in porch, even larger than the one at the other house. Laura Griffith wore blue jeans and a green t-shirt, her curly blonde ponytail making her look about thirty years old. She carried a plate with six huge ears of corn, cleaned and ready for the grill.

"Hey, you made it!" she said, grinning.

"We wouldn't miss it," Alex said before Etan could respond. Alex grabbed the plate, managing to give her a huge hug at the same time without any of the ears rolling off. "Thank you for shopping for us. That's a huge help."

"Well, I hate to come home to an empty kitchen after even a few days away," she said. She caught Etan in a hug that nearly squeezed the breath out of him. "I hope you have everything you need."

Etan shared a wink and a smile with Alex. Everything he'd needed after such a long, difficult drive had meant a couple of shots of the bourbon, the best sex they'd had in ages, and a long nap.

"We settled in just fine, thank you," Etan said. "This smells fantastic, Dad."

A little more silver than Etan remembered glinted in his father's brown hair when he turned away from the grill, but his smile flashed as youthful and joyful as his wife's had.

"Everything will be ready in an hour or so. Go grab yourselves something to drink, make yourselves at home." He hugged Alex, then Etan. "You *are* at home."

"I'm starting to feel that way," Alex said.

After they managed to carry huge plates of food, enough for at least a few more people, to the table on the patio, no one spoke for a long while. Etan was sure he'd grown up eating steak and potatoes and corn and tomatoes and butter this good, that he'd had it every time he'd returned for a visit over the last four years. But his nose and his mouth and his ravenous belly were certain nothing had ever tasted so good in all his twenty-two years.

"Can I ask you a strange question?" Etan said when he was finally able to slow down. "It's about the house, Gemaw and Grandpa's house."

"That's your house now," his mother said. "That's what they both wanted."

"Did they say anything about that?" Alex said.

"To tell you the truth, my mother did," Etan's father said. "She talked about keeping it up in case you needed it. Same thing with the car, Dad asked us to take good care of it. They didn't want things changed or updated unless they had to be. So that's why everything is a bit behind the times."

"Don't apologize," Alex said. He glanced at Etan before going on. "It's going to be just what we need, and the timing is perfect."

"Did she tell you why she wanted to leave it that way?" Etan said. He was sure he knew.

"Yeah, she told me she dreamed about it," his father said. "She wouldn't say much more, just that if you needed a place to stay, they wanted you to have the house. We've been using it as a guest house, but not very often. The place is yours for as long as you need it."

Etan tried to smile, but he couldn't quite manage. Alex put a hand on his leg under the table.

Alex had been right. This was it, where they would stay until the end. After that, even Etan couldn't yet guess.

"We appreciate that," Alex said. "We'll do whatever we can to keep up the place if you'll show me how. I'm afraid I don't have a lot of experience with house maintenance after years in apartments, but I'm happy to learn."

"I could use a refresher course myself," Etan said, gripping Alex's hand.

"I know this is hardly polite conversation," Etan's father said. "But I figure you're family, Alex, so you have to put up with me being as subtle as an ox just like Etan and Laura do. How are you two set for money?"

"We sold quite a few things before we left," Etan said. He didn't want Alex to have to answer this, not when he was already feeling bad about the lies he had to tell. Thanks to both of them being almost maniacal about savings, they had more than enough to last until money didn't matter anymore. "We'll be fine for a good long while."

"There are a bunch of other things I'd like to learn, speaking of money," Alex said. "Do you know anyone who still does a lot of gardening? Maybe preserving food?"

"Well, I haven't done anything like that for years," Etan's father said. "Mom and Dad insisted I learn how, but it does take up a lot of time."

"Time I have," Alex said. His cheeks were a little red, but he sounded okay. "I grew up in farm country, but neither of my parents gardened. I've always been curious."

"It really is too bad you didn't get to meet my father," Connor said. "He loved studying about self-sufficiency and growing things. His doctoral thesis was about pesticides and other advances in agriculture. How they helped, but the troubles around the turn of the century, too, how the bees were all dying off."

Etan met Alex's gaze, not even trying to hide his surprise. If he'd ever known that, he'd forgotten. He watched his father reach for another ear of the corn.

"Dad had a thing about certain crops, too, you'll find that in his writing. Things that were better or worse to grow out here." He waved the corn, now properly coated with fresh butter. "He loved fresh corn, but said we should enjoy it while we could. I never could work out why, but people around here hardly grow it anymore."

"There used to be a cannery in town," Etan's mother said, leaning back in her chair. "They shut down right after Anne passed. She and Evan really kept the place running. I know you remember, Etan, you were down there with them all the time. Everyone bragged about how good you were, even when you were little."

"Yeah, huge noisy place, but I loved it," Etan said, smiling a little. "I was afraid of all the equipment at first, then afraid they wouldn't let me go back if I acted up."

"If it's still in decent shape, maybe we can get something started," Alex said, staring into the thick trees beside the house. "Not a bad skill to learn or help other people learn."

His words left Etan dying to ask if Alex had dreamed for a change, if their late afternoon nap and lovemaking weren't the only things that led to such a change of heart.

"You remember Mom used to have a huge garden at your house and one up at the school," Etan's father said. "That's why we were always canning and putting stuff back. We couldn't eat it all, even after we gave a bunch of it away. I'm sure the soil is in good shape still. Dad had a ton of gardening books he bought, too."

"Yeah, I had a look at some of his books this afternoon while Etan was asleep," Alex said with a half-smile. "Seemed fair since he did all the driving. Might be a good way to get to know people, too."

Etan stared, trying not to laugh. He would have sworn Alex slept beside him the whole time, from right after they both collapsed in a sweaty, satisfied heap until Alex whispered him awake in time to get ready for this dinner. Instead Alex had used hours to himself to transform from scared to death in a strange place to eager to get out into the community, while Etan slept harder than he'd thought.

Alex's switch from anxiety to curiosity lightened Etan's guilt about dragging them into the unknown considerably.

"I know I'll feel a lot better once I'm busy again." Alex put his arm around Etan's waist, leaning against him for a second. "And I'll feel less like an outsider, you know?"

"Don't worry, you won't feel that way for long," Etan's mother said. "Anne always talked about how fast she felt at home here. I know you'll feel the same, Alex, as soon as people get to know you. We'll do everything we can to help, but you're going to do just fine."

Chapter 12

Etan jumped when he heard the front door open. He'd gotten so deeply into his grandfather's book about threats to pollinators, his grandmother's pink blanket tucked in around his knees, that he hadn't realized how much time had passed.

"Hey handsome," Alex said, walking through toward the kitchen with his arms full of paper bags. "Let me put these down."

"What have you got so much of?" Etan pushed the footstool aside and stood, stretching his arms over his head. The ceiling was low enough that Alex could easily reach it, but it was a few inches above Etan's fingertips.

"All the lettuce and spinach we'll ever need. My reward for asking around about food preservation. You'd be amazed how many people here have small greenhouses and gardens already. Now if we can just figure out how the hell to preserve it."

He put both arms around Etan's waist and buried his face against his neck. Alex's red hair smelled like rich, warm soil and fresh air.

"Freeze it, I suppose," Etan said. "Not very practical once the grid goes down."

"You have an excellent point there. I've found plenty of people who have gardens to go with those greenhouses I see everywhere, just hardly anyone doing much with them long term."

"Still no luck on the cannery?"

Alex leaned back with a crooked half-smile that warned Etan a second too late.

"I didn't say that. Your mother had the most amazing suggestion. She was a bit surprised you hadn't thought of it yet."

Etan shook his head and moved back toward the chair.

"Why do I get the feeling I've just been volunteered for something I'm going to regret?"

"Because you haven't heard me out," Alex said. He sat on the footstool and rubbed Etan's thigh. "She thinks we may be able to convince the high school to start classes out there again. Then it would be a legitimate school resource, so we'd have access to the funding to get it open and running."

"Sounds great. Now tell me the part I'm not going to like."

"That's the beauty of it, you *will* like it," Alex said. He was grinning, but Etan was somehow not reassured. "I'll do whatever I can to help get the equipment repaired and working. Might be my last chance to use my Engineer Alex skills before they get too rusty, assuming local folks will let the city boy mess with anything. As far as the rest, they just need someone to help get things set up, someone familiar with how it was run in the past. Keep up with paperwork and maybe write a couple of grants. Someone local folks will trust. You know, like Anne and Evan's grandson, recently come to his senses and moved back from the big city."

"Write grants? Paperwork?" Etan tried to get up, but Alex squeezed both of his thighs, pushing him back. "What makes either you or my mother think I could pull that off? Or that I want to?"

"Well, let's see. Your lovely mother—who's quite sure I'll be comfortable calling her Laura if she asks me often enough—was talking about how much you remind her of dear Anne. How you so loved going down there with your Gemaw when you were a kid. That's when the idea hit her. Since we're wanting to learn more, and Anne kept everything organized and enjoyed being out at the cannery so much, you're sure to be the best one for the job."

"I can't imagine anything I'd rather not do more than this!"

"So now that we're agreed on that first part, I'll tell you why I *know* you're the man for the job." Alex leaned forward, running his hands further along Etan's thighs. "You've been talking, asleep and awake, about how we're going to have to make a community here. How we'll never make it unless we help each other. What better way than creating a place where we can learn to take care of each other while we get to know each other better?"

"Fine, that makes all kinds of sense." Etan was trying not to want Alex to move his hands another little bit further without much success. "I'm losing the thread on the part where it has to be me."

"There's got to be a reason we came down here so early, E. Other people are going to show up, hopefully not too late. Now that I'm getting over the culture shock, I can see this will be a great place to do our best to make it through. But people even newer to this than us will have a hell of a lot of questions. We'll need a true community to survive. You're sitting in the middle of the best collection of the information we'll need within a hundred miles. This is a perfect way to start creating that community."

"No," Etan said. Much as he hated to, he grabbed both of Alex's hands and pushed them away. "That's not me. I'll learn as much as I can and help whoever I can, but I'm no social director. I hate that kind of shit, Alex. You know that."

"Don't worry, I'm not going to try to talk you into it. That never does any damn good anyway. You always kept our little household organized and on track a thousand times better than I could. I saw you do the same with a bunch of projects for school, too, and you never let anything slip. Whether you want to believe it or not, you're really *good* at that shit."

Etan stood up, stepped around Alex, and walked into the living room. He hated the suggestion almost as much as he hated the echo, the resonance in his belly. He rubbed his forearms, trying to ignore the hair standing on end. He knew Alex was watching him from the archway without having to look.

If he was going to live with this broadcast inside his head, one he hardly ever remembered when he was awake, he had to have the free will to disagree with it from time to time.

And if this community depended on *him* to create it, to bring it together, they didn't have a fucking chance.

He knew it was a mistake, but Etan turned to look at his lover. Alex was indeed watching him, leaning against the side of the archway with that same half smile. Nearly a thousand miles away from his home and in many ways even further from his career and life in Chicago, but trying his best to figure out their weird situation. Adjusting faster and more easily than Etan, even though Etan's dreams brought them here.

Alex was out in their new world like a grownup, meeting people and working out how to move them forward, while Etan still holed up at home and studied like a kid in school.

Was it really that much to ask, helping get this cannery set up? Especially when they both felt how important it would be to their survival?

Yep, looking into Alex's eyes was definitely a mistake. But Etan did it anyway. And he couldn't help returning Alex's smile.

Etan walked back and took his hand.

"I'll think about it, Alex," he said. "I'll help out, and I need to learn as much as I can. But I don't want to be in charge. I can't do that."

"You're going to like this suggestion even less, but just sleep on it. See what the middle of the night brings. Then maybe we can go talk to them in a couple of days."

Chapter 13

ALEX PACED OUTSIDE the white cinderblock building, shaking his head over being so early. He was half-annoyed at Etan for giving in to his agitation that morning and dropping him off more than half an hour before the time everyone had agreed upon. He'd also smiled, kissed Alex soundly, and refused to stay and keep him company.

Despite the key in his pocket, Alex felt strange about barging into an unknown space without anyone from town there. That left him wandering around the parking lot between the bulk of the red brick high school and the abandoned cannery at half past seven on a Saturday, like a demented stalker who'd lost track of the days.

Several windows interrupted the uniform white on the front of the building beneath blocky, faded purple letters declaring this the Wolf Branch Cannery. Alex hoped the windows were frosted, not just that horribly dirty. The steep, dark gray roof looked sound as far as he could tell. Double brown brick chimneys that seemed too large for the space rose on either end.

Steep mountains crowded close behind the high school buildings. The close-cropped grass of the football field and several baseball fields behind the cannery was still brown, the trees surrounding them barely flushed with pink buds. Plumes of pale smoke rose from many smaller chimneys throughout the town spreading out below Alex, matching the mist of his breath. He didn't think he'd ever get tired of the sharp wood smoke, welcome and strange to his city boy senses.

Even with the lingering chill, they'd have to work fast to get everything ready for early spring harvests, especially if the equipment inside was a mess.

He wore his own wide leather tool belt with a few of Etan's father's tools added to the jangling load. Alex hadn't had much use for big things like hammers or large crescent wrenches over the past few years, but Connor had insisted. He'd also insisted on the faded but well cared for clothes Alex wore.

Nothing Connor or Etan had would fit Alex's much larger frame, and his mostly business casual wardrobe was worse than useless now. So they'd dug into Evan Griffith's storage. The heavy blue jeans and long-sleeved dark blue denim shirt were almost a perfect fit. Both Conner and Etan had been happy enough about that to make Alex even more self-conscious.

Not only was he a stranger in this town, more out of his element than he wanted to admit in the privacy of his own mind, but he had to borrow another man's clothes to even pretend to fit in.

A dead man's clothes.

"Hey there," a cheerful voice with the slow local cadence called from the parking lot. "You must be Alex."

Alex turned to see a man taller than he was, but quite a bit thinner. He was probably in his sixties, gray hair mostly covered by a green baseball cap, body as lanky as his smile was friendly.

"Yeah, that's me."

"I'm right glad to meet you," he said, holding out a huge hand that swallowed Alex's. "Name's Walt Colley. I hated when this place closed down after Etan's folks did so much hard work to keep it going. Proud to help get everything working again."

"Alex Collins. Good to meet you, Walt. I'm hoping to help out a little bit, if you and the others don't mind."

Walt smiled, the effect like warm sunlight on an overcast day.

"Why on earth would we mind? We're needing to get more folks out here to work, not less. I'm sure you'll do just fine, Alex."

They walked over to the metal double doors. Conner had given him the key the night before, along with the same reassurances that he'd do just fine.

"Let's see what we've got to work with," Alex said, turning the key and pushing. The door didn't move.

"Naaah, you got to give it a good shove. Been locked up for years now, and never did quite work right." Alex stepped back, and the older man pushed into the door with his shoulder. The metal broke loose with a screech. "You and me can take care of that once we see how bad the rest has got."

Alex brought out one of Etan's many flashlights, borrowed with great reassurance that he'd bring it back home. Musty air assaulted his nose and sinuses. The light switch was to his right inside the door.

"There we go," Walt said when the lights flickered and sputtered.

Alex wanted to turn them back off and lock the door again. Only about half of the outdated long fluorescent fixtures were working, and the ones that were buzzed and burned at half strength.

They showed enough, though.

The big room, easily forty feet wide and sixty feet long, was dominated by two rows of huge stainless steel tables, all of them covered in what looked like equal parts dust and grease. Half a dozen gigantic cauldrons with a purpose he could only guess sat at the far end of the tables. Several silvery, square-bottomed cylinders with huge lids standing open, each large enough for Alex to bathe in, lined the opposite wall under more windows.

Deep square sinks were scattered throughout the space, along with various devices Alex couldn't even guess about. The only things he recognized were a few commercial ranges and ovens along the wall behind them, and at least those looked like they were in decent shape under all the filth. Massive steel storage shelves stood between two doors to the left, covered with enough pots and piles of utensils to supply a dozen houses.

"What a mess," he whispered.

"Yeah, take us a day or two to get this straightened up, I guess. We'll have more help directly, but we may as well take a look."

"I don't even know where to start."

Thick black metal pipes ran the length of the room under the peaked ceiling, with smaller pipes dropping down to most of the cauldrons and contraptions. A long metal grate down the middle of the gray concrete floor mirrored the overhead structures.

"I'm guessing there's a boiler or something," Alex said. "Do you know if it runs on gas or something else?"

"Gas far as I know, two boilers down in the basement. Just about everything in here runs on steam. We'll need to clear out those lines after so much time, make sure they're not gobbed up."

They walked around the vast room, Alex making mental notes of everything that had to be done. The problem was they really wouldn't know until they got the place cleaned up and tested the strange machinery. It was anyone's guess what was hidden under all the grime.

"Looks to me like all the equipment is sound," Walt said. He rapped his knuckle on one of the giant pots and grinned at the ringing bong.

"We can probably get it working if we don't run into too many big problems." Alex leaned down to get a closer look at six burners on one of the cooktops. "Might be a bigger problem finding people who know how to use all of this."

"That part's easy," a woman's voice said from the door. She was dressed as casually as Alex and Walt, in blue jeans and a stained old gray sweatshirt. Her hair matched the shirt, and it seemed desperate to escape the bun she'd wrangled it into. "Linda Burns. I was in charge of this whole operation, or the high school's part of it at least. Anne and Evan Griffith kept the whole thing running, really."

"Good to see you, Linda," Walt said, enclosing her small hand in his. "This here's Alex Collins. Just down from Chicago with Etan, Anne and Evan's grandson."

"Oh, I'm so glad to meet you," she said, taking Alex's hand in both of hers. "Etan knows a lot more than you think about how this all works. He was here with Anne all the time when he was a kid. Connor tells me you're a mechanical engineer?"

"I was before we left Chicago," Alex said. He hoped saying that in the past tense would stop hurting eventually. "I worked more with renewables than anything like this. Wind turbines, solar panels, that kind of thing."

"Hey, you're just the man we need, then," Walt said, grinning. "Most folks around here can rig something up like we have done all our lives, or manage to keep it limping along. Seems like we're going to need to do a whole lot better than that over the next few years."

A chill ran up Alex's spine. He was used to hearing such talk from Etan, awake or in the middle of the night. Walt seemed about as far from fanciful as a human being could get. Far from lying about something like that, too.

"What makes you say that?" Alex said.

"Nothing I can put my finger on," Walt said, but his cheeks were bright pink now. "One of them things you feel. Once you get to my age, you learn to trust that feeling."

"I know just what you mean, Walt," Linda said. She looked more pale than flushed. "After years of me begging for funds to make repairs to the classrooms I use every day and not getting one thin dime, suddenly the school board agrees to help us pay to fix this place up. I'm glad to have the money, sure. But I won't lie and say I don't wonder what changed."

"That's good enough for me," Alex said. "Sounds like we're about to have company."

Three men and a woman walked in, looking around in equal parts horror and anticipation. All of them were dressed and ready to work.

"This here's Alex Collins," Walt said before Alex could say a word. "Just down from Chicago, came with Etan Griffith. He's a mechanical engineer. Gonna show us how to get this place back on its feet."

Alex never got the chance to protest and declare his lack of fitness for the job at hand. His fears were swept away in the welcome and enthusiasm all around him.

He knew he had an intimidating, and exciting, amount to learn, and fantastic teachers eager to get started. By the time everyone made their introductions and they all took a closer look around the cannery, Alex was finally starting to believe he had more than a little bit to teach.

Chapter 14

EVEN THOUGH HE helped nearly every day for three weeks, Etan
was amazed at how quickly the cannery was ready to open. Six years
of neglect created an intimidating layer of dust, but not nearly as
much damage as Alex and everyone else feared.

A few days of hard scrubbing had the stainless steel tables, cauldrons for cooking down huge batches of fruit or vegetables, ranges,
and pressure canners spotless and gleaming. Alex and several local
folks, most easily old enough to be his parents, enjoyed every second
of talking and bullshitting while they worked.

Just as he had since the first night they'd met, Alex still transformed everything he touched. But Etan was determined he wasn't
going to fall neatly into line with at least a few of Alex's plans.

Every morning, he explained to Alex he was only going along to
help out, always including something along the lines of not wanting
to be in charge. Every morning, Alex grinned and said yeah, he knew
that.

And every day, Etan's high school vocational teacher Linda
Burns, Alex, and Etan's own mother asked him for advice over and
over again. Before long, the men and women helping with the
cleanup started to do the same.

The rhythm of the work, of the cannery itself, found its old place firmly under Etan's skin, inside his mind and heart.

Help Alex open the cool, dark building and start everything up for the day. Lights, boiler, steam lines that now worked better than they ever had in the past.

Welcome the ones who'd helped clean up and get the cannery as they arrived, carrying baskets and bags full of fruit and vegetables, often still dusty and warm from the garden. Breathe in the air as it slowly transformed from morning cool to afternoon warmth, humid and rich with the scent of cooking, then early evening muggy, with earthy but not quite unpleasant smells of human bodies.

Watch people walk out proud, with spotlessly clean and bright jars full of food, knowing at least that group understood how important their weeks of hard work getting the facility up and running had been.

Etan understood what was happening. He just couldn't quite manage to stop it. After a couple of weeks, even he admitted he didn't want to.

On the afternoon before the cannery officially opened, he caught Alex watching him. Etan stood surrounded by everyone who'd helped so far and several high school and middle school teachers, explaining his grandfather's planting schedule for optimum food preservation, crops they should focus on and some to avoid.

Alex's face was sweaty and smudged from his own work, but he wasn't even trying to hide his pride in Etan. Or his amusement.

Etan turned his back, flipped Alex off, and kept talking.

The truth was Etan was bursting with pride at what Alex had accomplished. His time here with his grandparents had been filled with clanking equipment, leaky pipes, boilers that required constant adjustment. Every bit of that and more faded into Etan's fond memories. More people than either of them imagined—or dreamed —wanted to do more than use the new cannery for more projects than he could easily keep up with.

Students and adults alike wanted to learn as much as they could, about updating their homes, putting in their own gardens, even filling out the grant applications Etan disliked almost as much as he enjoyed getting the award letters.

By the time early May crops of asparagus, beets, peas, and strawberries flooded into the cannery, both Etan and Alex were every bit as involved with the sprawling community garden next door as with paperwork and classes. After years trapped in the ongoing routine of college and studying, Etan enjoyed the labor more than he would have believed possible.

Maybe it was the deep, often dreamless sleep brought on by digging and weeding or hours spent in the steaming hot cannery. Maybe seeing what they'd accomplished only a few months after leaving Chicago with almost nothing built up his confidence.

Either way, Etan felt the smallest trembling optimism deep in his heart.

The catastrophe would strike, no doubt or way around that. But perhaps they had a chance of getting themselves and the others through to whatever awaited on the other side.

Another piece of their lives slipped gracefully into place.

Chapter 15

Mary Shadrin walked into their lives in July.

Etan caught motion out of the corner of his eye, looking up from a batch of strawberry preserves in an old-fashioned steam canner on one of the cooktops. He and a group of ten surprisingly attentive teenagers were watching the water boiling in the dark blue metal pot and listening to the finished jars cooling on the counter, waiting for the telltale pop of the cooling lids sealing themselves.

The scent of the remains of fragrant berries on the table behind him floated through the humid air, matching the perfectly ripe sweet flavor on his tongue.

He'd gotten used to the constant level of noise and humidity in the cannery faster than he'd expected. Clattering knives on other tables, churning or whirring machines, fragrant steam thick with early spring herbs. Etan's senses welcomed the comfort even though his grandparents weren't physically with him anymore. This place brought them close enough.

Movement that didn't match the general chaos distracted him. A small, slender woman with long, black hair stood in the open doorway, wearing a flowing blue gauze dress with open-toed sandals. Her features were delicate and severe, and he thought she was several years older than he was. Maybe closer to his parents' age.

Etan stared, trying to remember why he was sure he knew her, why she seized all of his attention. Something about her, besides those sandals that she couldn't wear with all the boiling and steaming in here, put his mind on edge.

"Was that it, Mr. Griffith?"

He turned back, searching through his memory of the last few seconds. Before he had to admit he hadn't been paying attention enough to hear anything, two more of the lids on the cooling jars compressed with a soft metallic *tink*.

"That's it. Anyone have your checklist?" Three of the kids raised their hands. "That's fine, I never had things like that with me when I was in school. Divide into three groups and go through your list. Make sure everything's set up. When they're all ready, start pulling them out. What are you watching for?"

"Anything that can burn the shit out of us?" one of the boys said, grinning. Despite his flippant attitude or maybe because of it, fifteen-year-old Jimmy Adams was one of Etan's best students. "Mr. Griffith, sir."

"Close enough, Jimmy. I'll be right over here."

The strange woman walked toward him when he turned back, and Etan held up his hands.

"I'm sorry, we can't let people wear shoes like that in here," he said. "Too many things at the boiling point. Can I help you?"

She stopped and crossed her arms

"I just wanted to see how things are going over here. We were all so disappointed when they closed down before. The previous managers died."

Etan did his best to smile. He noticed she was tapping one of her feet on the concrete floor, toe ring and painted red nails glinting. She followed him into the small office beside the double doors. With a fan in the only window on the street side of the building, it was a bit less humid.

"Everything's going really well, thank you. Pretty busy, but we have lots of help. I'm Etan Griffith."

She shook his hand with a satisfied smile. Etan was certain she'd known exactly who he was before she walked in.

"Mary Shadrin. Are you related to Evan Griffith? Or Anne?"

Etan didn't bother smiling this time. "The last managers. I'm their grandson."

"So sorry for your loss." Her expression didn't change.

"That was six years ago. I'm pretty much recovered. What can I help you with, Ms. Shadrin?"

"I just stopped by to introduce myself, Etan, and see if we can help you. My friends and I believe in being well prepared. Having this facility open again is a vital service to the community. A time of great need may be in our future, for us and for our neighbors."

"Well, I appreciate that," Etan said. He saw Alex waiting outside the office, dusty and hot from the garden. "We're happy to be here. Please tell your friends we're up and running, and they're welcome to come by."

"I'll be sure and do that."

Mary looked Etan up and down, glanced around the office, then turned on her heel and strode away. She made a show of scrutinizing Alex and his grubby, sweaty state on her way out. He wrinkled his nose and smiled as Etan reached him.

"Who the hell was that?"

"Mary Shadrin," Etan said. He looked out the doors, but the unsettling woman had disappeared around the corner toward the road. "Ever seen her before?"

"Don't think so. I think I'd remember someone that grouchy looking. I'm heading home to scrub my nasty ass. How long will you be?"

Etan glanced at his group. All of the remaining jars were out of the water, and the kids were milling around, looking his way.

"I'll be right behind you as soon as we finish up this batch," he said. "I'm reeky as a goat after sweating in here all day. If you can stand yourself long enough, I'll join you in the bath."

One of the few and welcome updates in their house was a huge soaking tub, one Etan's father had helped his grandfather install. There was more than enough room for himself and Alex, assuming they wanted any space to themselves.

"That's a date," Alex said, winking before he walked out. Etan rejoined his students.

"Three of them never popped, Mr. Griffith," one of the girls said. "The rest are cooling."

He'd given up trying to get them to call him Etan.

"Anyone know what to do with the ones that never seal?"

"Keep 'em in the fridge and eat 'em up fast," Jimmy said. The same one who'd suggested not burning the shit out of themselves.

"You got it. We'll let them cool down a bit, then do just that with the bread the last class baked. Help me clean up while we're waiting, and we're finished for today."

Etan meant to ask his parents about Mary. His attention got wrapped up with the kids and helping a few adults, then turned decidedly to Alex for the rest of the evening as soon as he got home.

By the time he remembered his plan to ask his parents about the disquieting woman, he didn't need to any more.

Chapter 16

ALEX WOKE WITH A START, certain he'd barely put his head on the pillow. One of those weird falling sensations he hadn't had for years must have jerked him awake. He was weary enough for that, between working at the cannery, helping build out a couple of gardens, and setting up a handful of small wind turbines over the past week.

An odd hissing noise in the darkness cleared the sleep from his brain in an instant. No, not quite like the snakes they'd disturbed in old garden boxes. That was Etan, shifting his legs under the sheets. Alex didn't remember any nightmares for a few days, but he didn't need to check the time. It would be just after three. The nearly six hours since they'd gone to bed had passed in a flash.

He jumped again at Etan's shout.

"Not you! No! Let me do it, *not* you!"

Alex turned on a dim bedside light, then reached into a tangle of sweaty, shifting limbs, twisted up in the sheets and blanket. Etan pulled away, groaning before his voice wound up into a scream.

"No one can save them!"

"Etan!" Alex caught Etan's hands and pulled, moving until he held Etan immobile with his own arms and legs. "Hey, I'm right here. It's okay."

Etan strained, his chest rising. Alex braced for another scream.

"Shhhh, calm down, sweetie," he whispered. "It's over now. I got you. You're safe. I got you."

Etan froze, then he shook his head.

"Not you," he said, his voice rough. "Let me, please."

"I'll let you, Etan, but you have to calm down first. You've screamed yourself hoarse."

Alex watched Etan's staring eyes, relief welling up in his belly when Etan finally focused on him in the faint light.

"There you are," he said, leaning down to kiss Etan's cheek. "You were starting to scare me."

"What's wrong?" Etan's voice sounded like he'd been to a concert or was just getting over a terrible cold.

"I don't have the slightest idea, E. You haven't told me yet."

Alex let out his breath, then moved onto his back. Etan followed him, curling up with his head on his chest. Shudders moved through him one after another, each one making Alex's heart ache.

He wished for at least the thousandth time that he could take the dreams away. Or at least take turns having them, give Etan a break from whatever demons he fought with in the night.

"Tell me your dream," Alex said. He pulled the covers over both of them. Etan was drenched in sweat despite the shivering.

"I don't remember. All I know is no one is safe. That keeps circling in my mind. No one."

Alex brushed back Etan's damp hair. "Safe from what? I'm not going anywhere, and no one else is here. We're both safe. Tell me about it so I can keep it that way."

"What did I say?"

"You were shouting. Not you, not you, let me do it. Then you screamed no one can save them. You've never had one that bad before."

"I can't remember what… No, that's not right. Almost everyone is dead." Etan squeezed tight, and Alex could almost see the dream ripping through his mind. "We can't stop them. A bunch more people going up there to die. In the higher mountains. They drink the water and turn into cartoons, stick figures. They bleed real blood, from everywhere."

"Do you know when?"

"How would I know when in a dream?"

This wasn't making sense. Alex couldn't tell if Etan was dreaming or awake. Etan rarely remembered his own dreams, not clearly. This sounded like one Alex would rather not know more about.

"Etan, are you awake? Do you understand what I'm asking you?"

Etan drew back, and his grip on Alex's arms loosened a little.

"Why wouldn't I understand? Of course I'm awake. I'm answering you."

Alex shook his head. "You answer me all the time after one of these. You hardly ever wake up all the way. You remember the dream, too?"

Etan shuddered one last time, then his body stilled and calmed.

"I still see them, crumpling away into dust. I don't know who I was shouting at. I can't remember, but I know I should."

"Listen, it's okay. If it's important, you'll dream it again. You do that all the time. If you don't wake up next time, maybe you'll be able to tell me more."

"I don't want another dream like that," Etan said. "The stick figures are worse than flesh and bone. I know how that sounds, but it's true."

Etan's heartbeat and breathing were almost back to normal, but now the images caught and invaded Alex's mind. What was coming toward them? Would he possibly be able to keep himself or Etan safe, much less anyone else?

"I wish I could make it stop forever, sweetie," Alex said. "Maybe I can for tonight."

Alex did stop the dream for both of them, with his mouth and his hands and his body.

But only for the night.

Chapter 17

The first rumors of food shortages drifted into town gossip late that October, right around the time everyone realized Wolf Branch had brought in a record harvest.

Etan's least favorite part of helping manage the cannery was the meetings, and this one felt a thousand times worse. Partly because it seemed like a thousand people were jammed into the high school auditorium, red and blue and green work clothes clashing with the purple and gold school colors around them. They'd hurriedly relocated from the cannery half an hour ago when it was obvious most of the town was showing up.

Five or six of them could usually stand around the gleaming steel tables, talk for a few minutes, maybe half an hour, then be done with it. Hardly anyone who didn't work with them seemed to care much about how everything stayed open, as long as it did.

The news—and rumors that grew from it—changed everything. Crop failures all around the country, from California to the Midwest to Florida, threatened to bring a nation long used to surplus uncomfortably close to rationing. The slowdown, some feared a new collapse, of the pollinators was impacting almost every staple food.

The weaknesses of a short, fast food supply chain only amplified the rest. Shelves didn't take a month to empty, or even a week. Shortages barely took days to get too big to ignore.

The same problems in different parts of the world kept food imports at their lowest levels in half a century.

In reassuring and sharp contrast, everyone's hard work had led to a huge surplus of food in Wolf Branch, fresh and put by. Reviving the food bank Anne and Evan were so proud of was the next logical step, but this harvest overran even those long ago plans and visions of helping people who were hurting for whatever reason.

Especially with the holidays and cold weather coming up, deciding what to do with shelves of canned fruit and vegetables along with refrigerators and freezers full of produce, meat, and dairy turned a quick conversation into a logistical challenge.

Etan sat in the back row of the auditorium with Alex, hoping no one would ask them to walk down the purple carpeted aisles to the stage in front. He still wondered if they should have kept this meeting secret instead of letting people know like they usually did. Folks were still wandering in out of the early time change darkness at ten past seven.

"What the hell are they all doing here?" Alex said, his arm around Etan. "We don't have that much food even if they did need it."

"It's more than that. They're hearing what's going on out there, finally starting to pay attention." He rubbed his tight shoulder muscles, relieved when Alex took the hint and took over. "Something worse tonight, though, not just the food. The first part of whatever we're going to face is about to land right in our laps."

"You've been restless enough lately," Alex said. He leaned close enough that his warm breath sent chills down Etan's legs. "I hope this lets both of us relax a little. We're overdue for some down time."

"Do you really think it will?"

Alex looked into Etan's eyes for several seconds. Etan saw the emotions chase across his lover's face, so much more out in the open than his own were. Alex was trying to hold on to his confidence, his assurance that they'd handle whatever came their way as long as they stayed close and worked hard enough.

And he was failing.

"I don't feel good about this either," he finally said, shaking his head. "We have to handle this right, all of us, or we'll have even more trouble down the road."

Linda Burns finally stood up at fifteen past, when all of the space behind Etan and Alex was filled with shuffling bodies. She constantly pushed the gray hair straggling out of her bun behind her ears and tugged at her green sweater. Linda was clearly used to speaking to a classroom full of teenagers, not hundreds of people in this packed auditorium.

"Thank you all for coming out tonight," she said. "We're a bit surprised, but we appreciate the interest. I guess you're here to help us decide what to do about the food bank and the surplus we have put by."

A rustle of whispered conversation passed through the room, but no one spoke out loud.

"When we did this in the past, we picked out a few families who were having troubles. That was just the easiest thing to do when we had extra. This year, we're going to have a lot left over after that. We were thinking of passing it along to other communities, other folks near us who might not have so much put by."

An older man near the front stood, pulling his faded green baseball cap off. Etan would be forever grateful to Walt Colley for working so hard with Alex, getting the mechanical parts of the cannery up and running. Even more for doing so much to help Alex finally feel welcome in their new home.

"I sure am sorry to interrupt you, Linda, but I imagine you been watching the news same as the rest of us. We might not be set up to pass anything along to another town. A lot of people are going to have trouble finding enough to eat this winter."

He paused, looking around, his face and ears bright red.

"I don't mean to sound so selfish, and it's not hardly Christian of me I guess. But we need to keep what food we can right here. We worked hard to end up with so much. We might need it before this winter's up."

Etan focused on breathing deeply, trying not to let himself get upset enough for anyone but Alex to notice. They were going to need a hell of a lot more food, and for a hell of a lot longer than this one winter. The way they made it through the next six months might set the course they followed into far worse trouble.

He still didn't feel like that was all that was happening around him, though. Something deeper, darker, moved through the huge crowd, keeping everyone as on edge as he was.

"We can sure talk about that," Linda said, raising her hands to try to quiet the crowd a bit. "I've been watching the news too. We're lucky we had such a good harvest here. A lot of the bigger farms and such struggled this year. I hate to hoard it all when most of us have plenty put back in our own houses."

"Most of us do, sure," said a small, dark-haired woman Etan didn't recognize, off to his left. "That doesn't mean we have to provide for people who didn't bother. Maybe they'll learn their lesson this winter and do better next year."

"Hang on now," Carla Phipps said from one of the chairs on the stage. She was one of the most tireless workers in the community garden. "I don't mean to be hateful, but I didn't see you doing a whole lot of work to build up the food bank, Crystal. None of us were before this year, to tell you the truth. If it weren't for Etan and Alex getting everything back on track and getting such a big community garden put in, we'd be hurting just as bad as all the towns around us."

Etan tried to shrink down in his seat, but Alex put an arm behind him. People were turning, looking for them, trying to put faces to the names if they hadn't already. Alex smiled, his cheeks flushed but unafraid. Etan thanked him mentally for not forcing them to stand up.

"Sure, we owe them a great debt," Crystal said, her face now red as the beets lining the shelves of the cannery. "We appreciate it, and I know Etan's grandparents would have been proud. But that doesn't change the fact that we *are* prepared. We worked hard to get that way. I still say that food needs to stay right here where we can get to it if the Food Lion ends up with even more empty shelves in January."

A smattering of applause floated through. Etan was relieved it wasn't louder, but he wondered if it should have been. He hated the idea of hoarding the food, especially if people only ten miles away were lacking. But he knew they had to get into this mindset, of understanding how important it was to plan ahead. Sooner might be better, even if it did feel like a horrible response to a worse problem.

"Well then, if you think we have to keep it, how do you propose we deal with that?" Carla said. She stepped up beside Linda, crossing her arms. "We're still busy putting this year's harvest away, and we'll run out of room before too long. Who's going to decide what to do with it when the time comes?"

"We might have to keep it back longer than we think," a woman said, standing near the middle of the crowd.

Etan couldn't see her face, and he hadn't heard her voice for months now. But he knew exactly who it was before she turned, making sure everyone in the room could see her.

Mary Shadrin.

Chapter 18

"We know you've been studying on such things for a long time now, Mary," Linda said. Her voice sounded calm, but even from the back row Etan saw the frustration on her face. He remembered it well from classes with her years ago. "One crop failure isn't the end of the world."

"It may not look like it from where you stand," Mary said, "with the key to months worth of food safe in your pocket. But we've been preparing for a long time now, getting ready for what's coming. If we decide this isn't that big a deal, that everything will recover in time, who are you going to for help when the whole thing crashes all around us?"

"What are you proposing, Mary?" said Joey Price, the preacher from the Episcopal church in town. He'd started a clothing drive to go along with the food pantry over the summer, so he sat on the stage behind Linda. "Are we supposed to ration food or something, when our neighbors are in need?"

"We're going to have to do exactly that," Mary said, her voice rising. She gazed more slowly at the crowd, and Etan would have sworn she picked him out without any effort at all. "You know we've been here for a long time, getting ready, watching the signs from all around us. This isn't just an isolated problem, Father Price. The food is starting to drop off all around the world."

"I think we can vote to keep this year's surplus," Linda said, trying to speak over the rumbling crowd. "But I'm not ready to say we're facing a worldwide crisis just yet. I know we can all work together to do more next year, especially with Etan and Alex learning and teaching us better ways to grow and preserve things every day."

The crowd again looked their way, but this time Alex wasn't so calm. He shrank back too, and Etan knew he was feeling that riptide current. The air was thicker, heavier. Things could turn against them, against all of them, before another heartbeat.

"I think they'd be just the ones to be in charge of the whole thing myself," Walt Colley said from the front row, still twisting his cap in his rawboned hands. "You're right, not a bit of this would be here if it wasn't for the two of them. They done a right fine job getting us ready for this winter. I say they should be the very folks to make sure we stay ready for the next one."

"This isn't right," Alex whispered, leaning into Etan's arm. "This isn't where we need to be."

"I say that's a fine idea," Linda said. She did what Etan dreaded, waving to them to walk up front. "If they'll join us and maybe say a few words, we can put it to a vote. We don't technically have to hold a vote of the whole town for something like this, but maybe we should hear what everyone else has to say."

"We can't do this," Etan said. "They'll rip us to shreds."

Etan's legs were made of lead, holding him to the seat. He knew if he tried to walk up to the front of the auditorium in front of what felt like an increasingly threatening crowd, he wouldn't make it more than a few steps.

Mary stepped in and saved him, at least from that much.

"Well, I propose they're *not* the ones who should be in charge," she said, her eyes flashing. "They've not even been back here a year, and one of them isn't *from* here at all."

Etan felt Alex go rigid against him. He gripped Alex's thigh, hoping he would be still. Etan had a terrible feeling they'd be lost if they spoke out now, especially if Alex let his temper get the best of him. He knew in his gut that this was not the right time for them to step forward.

"I don't see how that's relevant, Mary," Linda said, hands on her hips. "Sure, Etan was born in the hospital right here in town. But you need to remember his grandparents and his father weren't, and they did more for the community than most ever have. Alex is Etan's partner, and he's worked himself half to death helping everyone else out with the cannery and solar panels and windmills and everything else since the day he got here. That's all we need to know."

"I was born here, raised here, never have lived a day anywhere else," Mary said, her voice rising. "My friends can say the same, most of them. All of them have been here at least twenty years, getting ready. No one knows more about what's coming and what we'll have to do to survive it than we do."

Father Price stood, holding out his hands. "Mary, I just can't stand by and let you get everyone all riled up with this talk of some kind end times disaster coming." Etan felt Alex laugh under his breath, his tense muscles relaxing a little bit. "We can certainly listen to what you have to say, and we're glad to learn from you and your friends. But we're not going to turn everything we've worked so hard for over to you just because you want us to."

The crowd rustled again, and Etan felt the shift toward himself and Alex as clearly as if he'd seen flags moving in the wind. But that still wasn't right.

Having everyone, especially Mary, paying too much attention to them was the last thing they needed. Not now.

He hoped not ever.

"I suggest we have a voice vote," Linda said, holding up her arms. "We can get an idea how people feel, then we'll have something more formal later on. I probably should stay out of these things, but I've worked with Etan and Alex for the last several months, almost every day. I know they're good men, and I know I trust them. I say they should be the ones we're looking to at least until we know more about what's ahead of us."

A few people applauded, then more joined in a wave. Etan's flesh crawled with wanting to run, to get them out of there before the situation flew out of control. Mary whirled around, her eyes wide and staring.

Before the noise died down, she raised her voice to a shout.

"*I* am the one who can lead us into the future! *I* have seen where we're headed! If we don't correct our course now, we'll all end up in disaster!"

The silence hit hard enough to make Etan's head ache. No one moved, and he would have sworn no one was breathing either. It wasn't only Mary's words, shocking and strange as they were.

The air felt coarse, full of transparent gritty sand. It would be painful to try to move against the resistance.

Harry Mullins, a businessman who'd been in town his entire life, stood a few rows in front of Etan and Alex. His dark blue suit was terribly out of place among the flannel shirts and denim jackets, but Etan had never seen him wear anything else.

"Care to elaborate on that, Mary? You having visions now?"

"I have *always* had visions," she said, her voice harsh. "That's why I have the group of people around me, the ones who understand what we're going to be up against. I've seen more things come true over the last two years than I did in the twenty before. We are coming to the crossroads, and the wrong choice will be deadly to all of us!"

"Are you saying you hear from God?" Father Price said. He stood beside Linda, his hands now folded the same way they surely were on Sunday mornings.

"I don't need to hear from God. I see the future. I *dream* the future. And our future will be a nightmare if we do not make the right choices now."

A group of about twenty people stood around Mary, all of them nodding. No one else in the room spoke or moved. When she turned, her eyes fierce with triumph, Etan gasped.

"What's wrong?" Alex whispered, grabbing his hand.

Etan shook his head, too terrified to speak.

He didn't see the same woman, not even one as scary and possibly unhinged as Mary was right now. He saw eyes wild and lost, features gaunt, black hair streaked with gray. She stood with a different stance, not one of triumph, but one of bitter defiance.

No one made a sound, but Etan heard Mary's voice, hoarse with talking and shouting and screaming. He saw her raise a skeletal hand, pointing right at him.

"False prophet!" she said, the words booming and repeating through his head. The same crowd stood behind her, all of them equally unhinged and aged, echoing her in a terrifying chant. "Follow him to your death, to the death of all of us. We must remove the false prophet, cleanse him from our midst, if we're to survive. There is no other way forward!"

Time finally moved again, with Harry speaking to jar Etan out of whatever dream he'd been caught in. The horrifying vision of Mary was gone, replaced with her bright red face. Unlike most of his dreams, he saw and heard and remembered every detail of whatever had just happened to him.

"I don't want to be dragged into this kind of thing," Harry said, and now his own face was blazing. Etan saw he was sweating, even from so far away. "But this can't go on. Mary, I don't doubt that you have dreams. I don't doubt that they come true. The same thing has been happening to me for years now. And I'm not the only one."

The room erupted into noise then, and the temperature seemed to soar in an instant. More people stood, most of them shouting. Alex turned to Etan, eyes wide and terrified.

"What the fuck is going on here?"

"We must have some kind of order!" Linda shouted. "We can't turn into a mob, no matter what else is going on!"

After a minute of what sounded to Etan like pandemonium, but he was later sure was merely disorder amplified by his ragged nerves, people calmed down enough for Linda to speak again. Her voice was nearly as hoarse as Mary's had been in his hallucination.

"I don't know what to say, but we can't keep shouting at each other. Harry, do you have something else? Do you want to speak?"

Mary stomped toward the stage, fists clenched. She looked frightening, but back to being herself in Etan's eyes.

"I would like to speak! I am *not* finished!"

"For tonight you are, Mary," Harry said. He walked slowly up onto the stage, pulling out an absurdly old-fashioned white handkerchief and wiping at his face. "I don't know what the hell is in the air here tonight. But I do know you've said enough for now."

He stood in the middle of the stage. Despite towering over Linda at well over six feet, with barrel chest and broad shoulders to match, he looked for all the world like a nervous kid forced to give a speech for a class.

"I meant what I said. I've been dreaming about something happening, more and more all the time. I'm not going to call names, but I know I'm not alone. I'd sure appreciate it greatly if at least one of you would stand by my side."

Alex squeezed Etan's hand.

"No," Etan whispered. "Don't move. Don't make a sound. Please."

A few seconds passed, with Harry nervously mopping at his brow again. Finally several people got to their feet. Etan had seen all of them out at the cannery and working in the garden. Every single one of them had donated to the food bank or the clothing drive without being asked. Father Price joined them as well.

More people stood, and within a couple of minutes, twenty people stood beside Harry on the stage. At least that many more stood in the rows of seats. Etan could see Harry was still breathing hard, but the relief was a physical force in the whole auditorium.

"I don't know what all this is going to mean," Harry said. His voice trembled as if he was going to cry. "But it means the world to me for you to be here with me right now."

Mary stood again, but Linda stepped to the front of the stage, her hand on Harry's arm.

"I think we've all had just about enough for one night. We'll leave the food bank as it is for now. The same way it's been since Evan and Anne Griffith, who both grew up a long way from here, got it started for all of us."

"We got to bring the mayor and the town council in on this," Walt said. He stood not far from Harry on the stage, his hat now invisible in his red-knuckled hands. "I sure don't know what's happening, but we got to try to make sense of it."

"We'll do just that, Walt," Linda said. "I know a lot of you have a lot more to say, and we'll make sure that happens sooner rather than later. But for tonight, let's all go home and be thankful that we're arguing about having too *much* food to go around. A lot of folks in the United States of America might be in a different mess long before the spring comes around again."

Chapter 19

The tension in the room broken, everyone stood at once, turning toward the exits. Right toward Alex and Etan. After a few stunned seconds and increasing pressure on his hand, Alex realized Etan was trying to drag him to his feet.

"We've got to get out of here," Etan said. "Now, before it's too late."

They pushed through the crowd and out into the still empty lobby, moving at almost a run toward Evan Griffith's blue sedan they'd been driving lately. It started on the first try, just as the door to the auditorium opened.

"What's going on, E?" Alex said as Etan hit the gas a bit too hard going out of the parking lot. Gravel spun beneath the usually easy to handle car before he let off a bit.

"We can't get involved in this now," Etan said, shaking his head. "It's too dangerous. Everyone's too upset, and I don't want them upset with us."

"I think we're already involved, sweetie." Alex tried to take his hand, but Etan refused.

"No, I'm not just being stubborn or shy or whatever. This is not a joke. Something is wrong here."

Alex fought back a laugh that would have only made things worse. Mary Shadrin and everyone with her stopped just short of insisting she be put in charge, half the town outed themselves as dreamers, and all Etan could say was *something is wrong?*

"Explain it to me, then," Alex said. "I don't want to be in charge of some kind of sinister food rationing center either, but we *have* put a lot of this together. I doubt they'd have food to argue over if it weren't for us."

"I'm sure you're right, but you didn't see her face, Alex. She wasn't sane, not even a little bit."

"Mary? Aren't you overreacting? She seems a bit out there, but not dangerous. I did see her face. She looked like some kind of religious nut to me. What Harry said-"

"No, you didn't *see* her! She had... I could see something else there, something that hasn't happened yet. She's nowhere near as crazy as she's going to be."

Alex remembered to breathe when Etan slowed down, but not before the back wheels skidded sideways on the long curve at the edge of town. Running them over the cliff and onto the railroad tracks far below would at least bring everything to a quick end.

"You saw what? I don't understand what you're saying."

"I saw another version of her." Etan took a deep breath. "Her and everyone with her. They were all older, thinner. Her eyes were horrible. She was trying to get us put out or killed or something."

Alex scowled, pushing his hands flat against his thighs.

"Wait, are you telling me you saw that just now? Not when you were asleep?"

"That's exactly what I'm telling you. Please, let me get it out, I know it doesn't make any sense. I *saw* her, and I know it was her. Screaming, calling me a false prophet, saying I'd lead to the end of everything. Then it was gone."

"As clear as the dreams are?" Alex reached for his hand again, and this time Etan grasped his.

"More clear than the dreams are to me. I've only had a handful that I could remember at all. This was just like looking at her, like being in the same room with them just then. She's going to cause some kind of problem, one we might not live through."

"Don't you think we need to talk to someone about that, then?" Alex said. "Make sure she doesn't argue her way into getting put in charge of something?"

"No, we can't do that. I don't know what it is, but I know if we speak up right now, we won't survive it. She might turn directly against us instead of biding her time. I don't understand why, but I wasn't kidding about feeling like this will tear us to shreds. We have to let this work itself out. Please, please don't say anything, Alex."

After a few minutes of silence, Alex knew he'd stalled long enough. But he still couldn't work out what to say. What *could* he say about Etan having some kind of waking visions now, much less finding out they'd moved into a town half full of fortune tellers?

"I won't say anything," he said. "Not that anyone would listen. I'm the evil outsider. Not even from here, remember?"

"*Fuck* her and her fucking small town bigotry!"

Alex held his breath for a few seconds, trying to fight it, then he burst into laughter. The two of them laughed until they were both wiping their eyes.

"Tempting as that might sound to some," Alex said, "I'm going to pass. Do you understand what happened, Etan? A bunch of people have the dreams. Looked like half the town to me. I don't think she can hurt you with that many people having the same thing happen to them."

"I don't care, I can't be out there as a target. *We* can't be. That feels like a cliff under my feet, and one wrong step will pull you down with me. We have to wait it out and see what happens. What we're doing at the cannery is too important to risk. I can't let them know about my dreams. We have to keep our heads down. I got that loud and clear with the way she looked at me."

"I won't say anything, I promise," Alex said. He leaned against Etan's shoulder and whispered in his ear. "You're not the only one, E. Not anymore. You're not alone with this."

Etan shook his head, but when he glanced at Alex, he was smiling.

"That may take me a while to get used to," he said as he turned up the long road heading out of town. "Listen, we need to stop and talk to my parents. What happened tonight isn't going to stay a secret, probably already made it back to just about everyone here. We need to make sure they know not to say anything. They're not safe either."

Chapter 20

Etan's mother looked startled when she opened the door and saw them. Her hair was pulled back and she clutched a blue robe with pink flowers embroidered all over at her throat.

"What's wrong with you two? Did something happen in town tonight?"

Etan glanced at Alex, and both of them snorted out laughter before they could stop themselves.

"Yeah, you could say that, Mom," he said, fighting to keep the mad giggles from taking over. "Have you and Dad got a few minutes?"

"Of course we do. Did you two have dinner yet? I've got leftovers I can heat up in a couple of minutes."

Etan locked the door without thinking about it. When he met Alex's wide gaze, he realized what he'd done. He just took Alex's hand and kept walking.

"That sounds great, Laura," Alex said. "All this talk about food definitely hit me that way."

"We have company," she called into the living room. "He'll be out in a minute. Some kind of game on, but it's not baseball so I don't give a shit."

Alex laughed again, a normal laugh that didn't sound like it might take his breath. By the time they got settled at the table, Etan's father walked in. He wore sweatpants and a t-shirt so faded Etan wasn't sure what color it had been. Neither of them expected company so late.

"What brings you two out here?" he said. "Did you eat?"

"Mom's getting it right now," Etan said. "We just wanted to talk to you two about the meeting tonight. It won't take long."

"Something go wrong?" Etan's father said, sitting across from Alex.

"Something went strange," Alex said.

"What went strange?" Etan's mother said. She set two plates full of baked chicken, mashed potatoes, and green beans in front of them. Every bit of it from within a few miles of where they sat. "Husband, go fetch your sons something to drink. What do you want?"

"Beer would be perfect," Alex said.

"A glass of Mom's red wine might take the edge off."

A few seconds later, when his father returned with two of each, Etan was out of time. He was starving, and the food smelled amazing. But he knew if he tried to eat before he got this out, he'd end up sick.

"So what happened over there that got you so spooked?" his mother said. She sipped at her own glass of wine. "You looked awful when I opened the door, pale as a sheet."

"Mary Shadrin happened," Etan said. "What do you two know about her?"

"She's been holed up with a bunch of survivalists for the last fifteen years or so," his father said. "She was always an odd duck, worked as a psychic down in Asheville for a few years. That's gotten a lot worse since she brought a bunch of people back here to reinforce her crazy ideas. What did she do now?"

Etan tried to swallow a mouthful of potatoes without much success. Even his own parents thought someone else with the dreams was crazy. He'd been right to keep his mouth shut at the meeting.

"She tried to take over the food bank," Alex said. "Partly because she's seen a vision of the End Times Disaster to come. And partly because she couldn't tolerate a foreigner like me being involved."

"Oh come on!" Etan's mother said. Her light alcohol flush deepened into an angry one. "What the hell business of hers is it where you or anyone else came from? She was happy enough to cozy up to your grandparents when they were still alive, and neither of them were born here."

"Yeah, she mentioned them to me a few months ago," Etan said. "Said she was *so* sorry for my loss, wanted to see if she could help me down at the cannery. I told her to keep moving."

"You were right," his father said. "I've never trusted her, and Mom and Dad didn't either."

"Did they say why not?" Alex said.

"I got the feeling Mom dreamed about her, to be honest," Etan's father said. "And Dad always took that seriously. All of us did. She was always right about things like that."

"Well, apparently Gemaw wasn't the only one dreaming," Etan said, trying to smile. "Mary says she does, too."

"Bullshit," his mother said. "I'm sure she wished she could tell the future, or at least that people would believe she did. But she never said a word about anything like that."

"She's not the only one, Mom," Etan said.

"I know you always did," she said. "That doesn't mean...I don't want you to think we think you're..."

"It's okay. I felt that way myself for a long time," Etan said. "Until I met Alex, really. Harry Mullins stood up and said he has the dreams too."

Both his parents stared at him without saying a word, their eyes so large he had to once again force himself not to laugh. He finished his wine instead and poured more for himself and his mother.

"A bunch of other people too," Alex said. "I think it was about forty. They backed Harry up and made Mary shut up. I get the feeling she's not finished, though."

"They all said that, in front of everyone?" Etan's mother said. "I never even heard Anne say that in public. She never hid it from your father, or from you, of course. But she kept it to herself otherwise."

"That's what we're going to have to do now," Etan said. "I saw something else strange tonight, first time that's happened to me. Am I remembering right that Gemaw saw things while she was awake sometimes?"

His father nodded, a sad smile on his face.

"She didn't talk as much about that as the dreams, but she told me that, yeah. She said she saw how people were going to die, over their faces like a mask. She had times when the only face she could see clearly was Dad's."

"Jesus," Alex said under his breath. "Her whole life?"

"Started the same time as her dreams did," Etan's father said. "I think that was the hardest thing for her. That's probably what led to a lot of her trouble, even more than the dreams. Is that what you saw tonight, Etan?"

Etan's heart twisted at the worried sound of his father's voice, surely remembering stories about how badly his own mother suffered.

"Not how Mary's going to die, no. I think I saw how she's going to end up. What she's going to try to do. Whatever problem she has is going to get worse."

"Etan said she would try to get us killed," Alex said. "If anyone finds out about his dreams right now, that's where we're headed."

"Trying to get you killed?" his mother said, her eyes flashing. "That's enough. Time to tell Sheriff Grant about this."

"No. Please, don't do that," Etan said, leaning forward. "You said there were times when Gemaw saw things you ended up believing, right? Was it ever anything like this? When she asked you to keep quiet when you didn't want to?"

"There were a lot of times like that," his father said. "Times when Dad told me something she dreamed about, but she didn't want any of us to do anything about it. Some things I've never yet told anyone about. She was right. Every time."

"Well, I believe Etan is right, too," Alex said.

Etan loved him more than his own life in that second.

In every second.

Even in the house he'd grown up in, the resistance was as thick and painful as it had been in the auditorium. Etan had never requested belief in his visions, much less demanded it. Alex had simply offered that belief, with no idea what he was doing, to save Etan's sanity months ago. And both of their lives in the months ahead.

Right now, he knew he had to expect the same from his parents, demand if he had to. That was the only possible to way to keep all of them safe. He was terrified he'd demand the same belief from everyone around him before another five years passed. But not now.

"I can't explain this any more than I can explain why we had to come back here when we did," Etan said, grasping Alex's hand. "But I know we have to keep our heads down. Things are going to change in the future, but if we get pushed in the middle of this right now, everything is going to fall apart. We won't be able to stop Mary or anyone else."

"I've never trusted Mary or anyone who's with her," his father said. "You two still have a gun up there?"

"We have a gun," Alex said. "I haven't handled one since I was about ten years old, and that wasn't for long. I'm afraid I'd shoot my foot off."

"I don't like this business of Mary or anyone else making threats against you two," his father said. "But I'll let it go for now, if you let us make sure you both know how to defend yourselves. I doubt she or anybody else with so goddamn much bluster will be brave enough to come up here. If they do, though, make sure they understand exactly why they need to get the hell out."

"I haven't shot in years," Etan said. "Not since I moved to Chicago. I was pretty good at it back in the day. We might be able to train Alex up enough to be at least passable."

"Good luck with that," Alex said. He didn't sound afraid, though. He sounded excited.

"Your grandmother always dreamed about the world coming to some kind of hellish end," Etan's mother said. She'd finished her second glass of wine as well, but Etan knew the flush in her cheeks didn't mean she was the least bit drunk. "Is this why you started up the cannery and the food pantry, Etan?"

"Yeah, that's part of it," he said. "Same with all the power systems Alex is setting up. That's not gonna be enough. Not nearly enough. But we had to start somewhere. I'm sorry we haven't told you more of this before now."

"Well, you're telling us now," his father said. "You and Alex have done wonders for this community in such a short time. If Mary or anyone else can't see that, or if they resent it, they're even crazier than we thought."

~

THE FOOD SUPPLY held out through that winter, at least in the developed world. Many parts of the planet were not so lucky.

People who did have enough understood it was a near thing, nearer than it had ever been before. They worried things would get worse in the future.

Before another year passed, every person on the planet understood how far off their most dire predictions had been.

How mild their deepest fears.

Humanity would never again have so lofty a goal to fail as enough food for a modern world.

Chapter 21

T HE BASEMENT of the cannery seemed like the worst place in town for storing anything the first time Etan saw it. Less than an hour of poking around the musty and dank space, an ominous boiler at either end, the middle filled with broken equipment that had probably been down there since before he was born, sent him rushing home for a hot shower that day.

Another huge spring harvest, along with whispering fears of nearby towns finding out about their growing food surplus, sent Alex and his dedicated crew of amateur engineers down to clean the place up.

By the time they finished in mid-August, the basement was as bright and clean as the grocery store in town. Alex even managed to add another class to what he was already teaching high school kids and adults. Along with working with solar panels, wind and water turbines, and batteries, people learned how to install a generator to run the lights and ventilation fans, one that ran on gasoline or fuel alcohol. They finally had a use for the piles of sugar beets everyone was able to grow, and a reason to set up legal distilleries out in the open for everyone to see.

Walt Colley looked up from where he was helping Etan count the latest batch of donations, several cases of canned goods.

"Hey there Alex," he said with a slow smile.

Etan turned to see Alex looking over his shoulder as he hurried down the new wooden steps, buckling his brown leather holster around his waist. Etan couldn't remember when he'd last seen Alex carrying his gun when they weren't practicing shooting. His normally open and happy face was tense and grim.

"Hey Walt," Alex said. "Everyone needs to get upstairs. I don't want them seeing how we get down here."

"Who?" Etan said. "What's wrong?"

Alex pulled his green work shirt out of his jeans to cover up the holster, but not before everyone in the room saw it.

But Etan was more alarmed by his father's face than his lover's words. Connor Griffith steadied himself with one hand against the white cinderblock wall, his face nearly as pale.

"I don't know where they're from," Alex said looking up the stairs again. "Hope I'm just being paranoid, but let's go. Come on."

Alex starting turning off the lights before everyone made it up the stairs. Etan touched his father's shoulder as he passed by, but he just shook his head. Alex's back felt like vibrating wires under Etan's hand.

"What the hell's going on, Alex?"

"Several big pickup trucks drove into town a little while ago," he said. "Gun racks fully loaded and on display. We should have help in a few minutes."

Etan followed Alex up the stairs, watching him lock the door behind them. No one ever did that until they locked up the entire cannery at night.

Everyone was gathered around the frosted windows overlooking the parking lot by the time Etan got upstairs, peering through the open edges. Linda kicked the rubber stop away from one of the double doors.

"No," Alex said. "We're not going to lock it with all of us standing here in plain sight. We need to hear what they want and not let them know we're afraid. Everybody stay calm."

Three men and a woman, their own firearms clearly visible, walked toward the door of the cannery. Etan had never seen any of them before. Several others stood beside their huge antique pickups in the parking lot.

"Don't just stand here staring," Etan said, taking a few steps back himself. "If they didn't come looking for trouble, this is the best way to make sure it starts anyway."

Everyone managed to be busy by the time the three strangers got to the door. Etan walked back over, hoping his shaking hands didn't give them away. The four of them looked normal enough, all wearing work clothes just like anyone else in town. He had to bite back a laugh at the faded blue and red kerchiefs they all had pulled up over their faces, like redneck caricatures of an Old West museum exhibit.

Etan had the strongest feeling this was beginning of trouble that would not be over that day.

"Good afternoon," he said, trying not to cringe at his own nervous formality. "Can I help you?

"Afternoon," one of the men said in a slow drawl. He was taller than Alex or even lanky Walt Colley, with wavy gray hair that fell to his collar. The woman beside him, her graying blond hair pulled back in a ponytail, was nearly as tall.

"We hear you been doing good things over here," he said. "So we figured we'd stop by and say hello."

The other three didn't say anything, but their eyes never stopped moving, looking over all the people and equipment in the steaming hot room.

"We just got opened back up last year," Alex said, stepping up beside Etan. "Figuring out how everything works, teaching a few classes at the high school."

"Quite a garden you have put in out there," the man said, waving his hand toward the door. "Making good use of the harvest?"

"Same as with the cannery," Etan said. "The main thing is making sure the high school kids know how to grow things and take care of themselves. Having a problem with dust where you came from?"

"Just trying to keep healthy. Never can be too careful these days with all the trouble out in the world."

"We'd be glad to help you set up a program for your own kids," Linda said. "Did you come from close by?"

"Close enough," the man said. "I get the idea you had quite the surplus last winter. How's that looking for this year?"

"Not as much as we'd like." Alex leaned against a metal table and crossed his arms. "We're all doing the best we can to get ready for another rough winter."

A huge clatter made everyone jump, and Etan turned with his heart pounding. His father crouched beside a huge pile of pots and utensils, red-faced instead of pale, trying to disappear into the concrete floor.

When he turned back, the other men and the woman had taken several steps toward the middle of the room. Alex moved forward.

"We're only in for short hours today," he said. "We'd be happy to talk to you about setting something up where you came from. Right now we're about ready to lock up and go home."

"We'll head out here a little while," the woman said, walking toward Connor and the pile he was still cleaning up. Uncomfortably close to the door down into the basement. "We'd sure like to hear more about that surplus you had last year. How that's holding up?"

"Just like anywhere else I suppose," Alex said. He shifted his hand to the gun hidden under his shirt. Etan would have sworn he heard Alex's muscles thrumming. "Working hard to make sure we have enough to feed our families."

"Where you finding to keep your stores?" the woman said.

She continued her slow walk around the room, taking notice of everyone pretending not to notice her. Alex watched her more closely than the others.

"I'm starting to think the Sheriff's office might be the best place," Etan's father said. He looked horrified at the words that had just come out of his own mouth.

"Is that right?" the first man said. He walked up beside Connor, standing easily six inches taller. "Pretty goddamn easy to be cocky when you're sitting on enough food to feed your families and a bunch more besides."

"I think we're just about done here," Walt Colley said in the loudest voice Etan had ever heard from him. "Hiding your faces, strutting around like you own the place. Unless you all have something useful to say, about time you head outta here and quit bothering us."

Sheriff Grant and two of his deputies walked in before anyone else could speak. None of them looked the least bit tense or upset. Just out for an afternoon drive, decided to stop by for a visit. Alex caught Etan's attention and winked.

"Looks like you got quite a crowd in here for a short day," Sheriff Grant said. He stood with his arms relaxed at his sides, nowhere near the handgun on his belt. But Etan couldn't stop himself from realizing they now had as many guns as the strangers, and three officers well-trained to use them.

"I believe our visitors were just about to head out," Alex said, standing by the doors. "We sure wish you all the best of luck with your own harvest."

The strangers turned slowly, looking at each of them in turn. The tall man met Etan's eyes for several uncomfortable seconds. The woman's gaze, emotionless and flat, chilled him to the bone. She jerked her chin toward the door, and the others fell in line behind her.

"We certainly did have an informative visit," the tall man said as he walked toward the door. "I'm sure looking forward to when we cross paths again."

When they passed through, Alex closed both doors and turned the deadbolt.

"Thank you for getting over here so fast," Alex said, shaking hands with the sheriff. "That settled them down, at least for now."

"We did a little checking on the way over here," the sheriff said. He shook Etan's hand, too, and clapped him on the back. "This wasn't the first place they dropped in to, hokey handkerchiefs and all. They haven't caused any real trouble yet, but they're making it clear they'd like to."

"Where the hell are they from?" Etan said. Now that the strangers were gone, he was shaking and covered in sweat.

"Well, they've got fake plates on their trucks," Sheriff Grant said.

"Antique gas models, no tracking sensors. Can't see enough of their faces to recognize even if we did know them, which is just what they wanted. They haven't done anything we can arrest them for or even make them admit who they are without causing a lot more trouble. Everyone I talked to has their hands too damn full to follow them home right now, same as we do."

"You got any security set up over here?" Deputy Wiggins said. Etan thought her first name was Melissa. "Alarms or anything like that?"

"Nothing besides the basement and locks on all the doors," Etan said. He walked over to Alex, thankful for the warmth of his arms. "Those days might be over."

"We'd be happy to keep an eye on the place for you," the sheriff said. "But if they're out looking for an easy target, best thing may be to make sure you don't give 'em one."

Etan's stomach sank at the thought of arming themselves against their neighbors, though his heart and what Alex told him about the dreams let him know that was the next step. Modern security systems would be useless before much more time passed, but they couldn't ignore the threat. Alex squeezed him and rubbed his shoulder.

"We'll talk to the school administration about it," Alex said. "It's probably time to move everything out of the food pantry in town as well. I'm afraid this winter's going to be a rough one."

When the sheriff left, Etan helped his father with the last of the cleanup.

"What's going on, Dad? You look like you're about to pass out, then you just about dared those goons to start shooting."

"I know, I'm sorry. I couldn't stand by and let them threaten you and Alex. You're too important to risk."

"So are you, old man," Alex said, smiling and helping both of them to their feet. "You grew up here, Etan. Is there a basement under the high school we could use instead of the food pantry? That would be a hell of a lot easier to secure than the old building in the middle of town with those huge windows."

"Yeah," Etan said, still watching his father. He seemed fully recovered if a bit shaky. "The basement's at least as big as the whole building. They had classrooms down there when I was in school. We could turn it into a ton of storage space."

"Mary and her cronies aren't going to like that idea," Linda said, leaning on the storage shelf. "They're still saying we all have to work together, that we need to share all our food and ration it so we can help everyone."

"Sounds like a great way for all of us to starve," Connor said. "They've been talking to a lot of people in town, though."

"We're going to have to do the same," Linda said. "And we may just have to get our stores moved without Mary and her followers finding out about it."

Alex looked at Etan, his brow creased, his blue eyes worried. Etan knew they were thinking the same thing that neither of them were willing to say.

All the hiding in the world wouldn't stop dreamers from knowing the truth.

~

SMALL GROUPS STARTED STRAGGLING in as the weather turned cooler. Several were returning home much like Etan had. A growing number followed dreams to a small mountain town they'd never heard of before.

They settled into houses long empty, breathing a bit of life into Wolf Branch after years of quiet decline. Almost everyone showed a quick interest in growing and preserving food, drawn to the cannery and community garden as if by magic.

Even as the outside power grid supplying Wolf Branch weakened and grew more erratic, the new arrivals adjusted with enthusiasm and relief. Too many to be a coincidence brought equipment they didn't know how to use with them. Precious space and resources taken up with glossy solar panels, small water and wind turbines, boxy storage batteries.

Neither they nor Alex and his growing crew of installers were surprised to find themselves in the same small town.

The influx continued as news from around the world worsened over the fall. The harvest was better worldwide, but stores depleted by previous winters in both hemispheres were still terribly low. Shipments were more erratic, leading to many things disappearing, then reappearing sporadically.

Fear of worsening riots joined fear of starvation, and those fears became reality far too often.

One of the last large groups to arrive in Wolf Branch captured all of Etan and Alex's attention. A doctor bringing years of emergency room experience along with years worth of medical supplies replaced their worries about people getting hurt or sick in the future with worries about how to keep the priceless medicine and equipment safe in the growing uneasy climate all around them.

Mary and her followers found out about the community's growing supplies, and where they were stored, through their own magic.

Chapter 22

THE SPACE under the high school was larger and more useful than Alex expected, and much cleaner than he'd feared. Unlike the neglected mess under the cannery, the maze of rooms, hallways, and closets was mostly empty. Everyone who'd been there for the disturbing masked strangers' visit to the cannery pitched in, and the whole space was clean in a few hours.

Shrinking class sizes left this part of the school abandoned a few years ago, but Alex couldn't help imagining Etan trudging through the purple and gold tiled hallways. Maybe when they got home from this late night supply run, he'd ask his lover about that.

He walked up the narrow concrete steps, playing the scenes and questions out in his mind. Was your first kiss with a boy or a girl? Where was it? Alex stepped out into the quiet November night, grinning to himself.

Did you ever have sex down in that basement?

Whether Etan ever had or not, Alex definitely thought the two of them should.

"Working late, Mr. Collins?" a woman said. He couldn't see her face where she stood in the shadow of the building, but he knew her voice.

"Not working at all, Ms. Shadrin. Just cleaning up for new classes. What brings you out this time of night?"

She stepped toward him, the security light Alex had installed a few days ago showing her narrowed eyes and pursed lips. She was wearing dark pants and a dark jacket, and her hair was pulled back. He'd never seen her dressed in a way to avoid attention rather than her normal flowing pastel wardrobe.

"Even with all these newcomers, there aren't enough students to open up that basement again," she said. She glanced toward the big enclosed truck they'd been using for these nighttime runs, rescued from a previous life as part of a delivery fleet. "Looks like a lot of cleaning supplies for one building. Strange that you feel the need to lock up a bunch of mops and brooms."

"Like you said, we've had a lot of new arrivals over the past few weeks, and their kids need school as much as anyone else. Strange that you're so worried about the high school basement."

"Is this where you're hiding the food, Mr. Collins?" She crossed her arms. "The food our town and our neighbors need so badly?"

"I'm not in charge of the food or the cleanup. You'll have to talk to Linda Burns about that. She's pretty damn busy with teaching and helping run the cannery. And if you're going to accuse me of hiding anything, drop the mister nonsense. My name is Alex."

"I fully intend to speak to Linda, once she shows some courage and stops avoiding me. I have a voice as part of the town council. Linda and a few others need to remember that."

"We're all well aware of who's on the council," Alex said. "That has nothing to do with what we do here at the school or at the cannery. You're on the wrong track here."

"If you're not hiding food down there, I'm guessing that's where you keep the guns. Robert Phillips dreams about them, night after night. The dreams are coming to me, too. These weapons you cling to will lead to a slaughter, one neither we nor our neighbors can afford as the end draws near."

Mary walked toward him, stopping a few inches away. She smelled flowery but a little too much, like she'd been rolling in an overripe flower bed.

"I know you're a reasonable man, Alex."

"No, Mary. You don't." Alex shrugged and leaned against the cool bricks, arms crossed. "You don't know anything about me at all. Let me give you a hint. If you continue to interfere with our work here, I'll get downright *un*reasonable."

"Maybe Mr. Griffith will listen to me then," she said. "Connor, I mean. He might not have graduated from this school like his son and I did, but he's lived here for thirty years."

"Like I *haven't*, right? Something else you should know about me, since you're so fond of saying I'm not from around here to anyone who will listen. I'm happy to play the perfect big city hothead you seem to expect when the situation calls for it. Damn good at it, too. If you or anyone around you bothers my family, I won't just be unreasonable. I'll be pure hell to deal with. Got it?"

"You have not yet seen the hell we'll all have to live through because of such arrogance! We'll be lucky if anyone lives through it at all."

"I suppose we'll all find out when the time comes," Alex said. He and Mary both turned at the sound of voices in the stairwell. "Right now all you're accomplishing is keeping us from doing everything we can to make sure we survive."

"We *will* find out, Alex." She walked toward the curving asphalt road heading into town. "I hope none of you does anything you live to regret. If you live at all."

Chapter 23

Sandy Hughes, another returning native of Wolf Branch, brought the truck full of medical supplies south from Chicago. She made no attempt to hide the dreams that brought her back to her birthplace. A hectic week spent storing and arranging everything Sandy brought ended with dinner with Etan's parents.

"How did you get all the supplies out of there?" Etan said.

"No one's really paying attention anymore," Sandy said. Her dark blond hair was caught back in a thick braid from the workday, and she still wore her faded and patched coveralls. "They're too busy trying to keep up to watch things like medical supplies walking on their own."

"We figured the government is keeping a lot of things quiet," Alex said. "And most people would rather not know anyway."

"I wish I didn't know about most of it," Sandy said. "Bigger sections of the city than you'd believe are empty, but I just about waited too late to get out. Some of my friends who got out a lot earlier barely made it."

"What's happening?" Etan said. "Is it still safe to travel?"

"I wouldn't go back up there," Sandy said, shaking her head and sitting back. "Takeovers of links in the food chain started a while back. State and federal government so far, but that's not going to last. The police are so busy with trying to protect supply trucks that they're not able to stop raids and attacks on grocery stores and warehouses. Every time something disappears, then shows back up, the whole cycle gets worse. Traffic around cities is getting worse, too, and roads are falling apart."

"What about north of Chicago?" Alex said, his voice quiet. "Around Wisconsin."

Alex had never been particularly close to his family, but Etan had heard several phone calls trying to convince his parents and brother and sister to join them. They seemed determined that the trouble wasn't going to be as bad as most people said.

Etan and Alex both knew it was going to be worse than most people imagined.

"I'm afraid it's bad where it's colder, Alex," Sandy said. "Most of the roads didn't get repaired after last winter. A lot of supplies never made it up there, either. Illinois was bad enough. I can't imagine how bad it's going to be in Wisconsin."

Alex grunted, then rubbed his eyes.

"How's the hospital in town looking?" Etan said.

He wanted to get Alex focused on something else. Something he could actually make better.

"It's outdated, certainly compared to the teaching hospital I left behind," Sandy said with a lopsided smile. "We'll be able to handle the basics here. The much smaller building will be a lot easier to manage, really. As long as the power holds out."

"Alex is your man, then," Etan's father said. Whether from his own sense of future events or from simply paying attention, he hadn't missed Alex's mood shift any more than Etan had. "He got the cannery and a bunch of other places set up with their own power."

"Using gasoline?" Sandy said.

"Some of the generators can, yeah," Alex said. "They're all capable of running fuel alcohol when that dries up. Good bit of solar wherever we can fit the panels, small wind and water turbines. I keep hearing there are a lot more big turbines up on Maple Ridge that should be keeping the power more consistent than it is, but I haven't had a chance to go up there yet. Batteries for storage here in town, but never enough of those."

"Alex set up good old-fashioned stills to take care of the fuel," Etan's mother said. "Not a thing goes to waste, and we'll be able to grow what we need."

"Interested in helping me out with power at the hospital, Alex?" Sandy said. She pulled a tiny spiral notebook out of her back pocket. "I've been wondering how we're going to handle everything once the grid goes down."

"For a building that size, we need to look at the river," Alex said, rubbing his chin through his beard. "It's just a few blocks away. We have bigger water turbines I haven't set up yet. We could keep running water, too, at least for a few buildings. What kind of power are you going to need?"

"As much as you can get me. Mind if I steal your husband for a couple of months, Etan? I promise to send him back as good as I found him."

Etan looked into Alex's blue eyes, now sparkling with the prospect of a huge new project to dig into. And at least for the moment, no longer sad and worried about the family he'd left behind.

"Keeps him out of my hair, so that's fine with me."

"Etan hasn't made an honest man of me yet, anyway," Alex said. He winked at Etan. "I'm still a free agent."

"I've been meaning to ask you about that, boys," Etan's mother said. "People are starting to talk, and I'd love to help plan a wedding while we still have the chance. I think early December would be the perfect time for a party."

Etan lowered his head, looking at Alex out of the corner of his eye. He remembered silvery wedding rings from a few dreams. From the first night they'd spent together, the first moment they'd met, he'd always assumed it would happen.

He'd never considered the timing.

"What do you think, Alex? Might be your last chance to trade up before the end of the world."

"Twenty-six is too old to ask me to change my ways," Alex said. He was smiling, but Etan was surprised at how bright his eyes were. "You'll have to do."

Chapter 24

Alex paced around the basement of the Episcopal church, his gleaming black shoes silent on the tan carpet. He could hear people walking around up in the sanctuary. Too many people. Far more than he and Etan planned for.

The borrowed black suit fit him surprisingly well once Linda asked the crafts teacher at the high school to alter it for him. He wondered how Etan's had turned out. He'd find out in a half hour or so, if his nervousness didn't stop his heart before then.

What the hell had he been thinking, agreeing to antiquated notions of not seeing each other before the service? Alex doubted those superstitions ever applied to two grooms in the first place.

They were already racing to beat the end of the world. Bad luck coming up seemed to be a given.

He grinned and shook his head, then glanced down at his watch. A beautiful gold model with a black leather band, something else borrowed for the occasion with supplies of such luxury items or fabric for new suits almost impossible to get now.

Twenty-one minutes to go.

Plenty of time to get himself good and freaked out when all he was doing was marrying the only person on earth who could have suited him so perfectly. That outran a hell of a lot of bad luck.

Alex kept pacing.

The long tables throughout the huge basement, the space of the whole church above and then some, were set with more places than he wanted to pay attention to. People had brought their own plates, bowls, and silverware, but the unintended patterns of colors, shapes and sizes appealed more to his eye than bland sameness ever could have.

Plans for a quiet service at the town hall evaporated before they ever got started. Between his soon to be mother-in-law and just about everyone else he'd met in Wolf Branch, Alex was sure the entire county would be in attendance.

No one from his own family would.

There was only so much he could do. Even if he and Etan had made the increasingly dangerous trip back up north and attempted to physically put them in the van and head south, none of them were going to leave Fond du Lac. That terribly risky effort with bad weather underway would certainly have ended in tears and a heart-broken journey back to Wolf Branch without them. Alex shook his head, trying to dislodge the thoughts before they could dig in and spoil his pleasant, nervous anticipation.

A door behind him creaked, and Alex jumped. He was more anxious than he thought.

Walt Colley walked toward him, for once not gripping his faded green baseball cap in his massive hands. Walt was as nicely dressed as Alex himself. He wore a lovely dark gray suit, a few tiny flowers from the greenhouse they'd built not that long ago pinned to the lapel. Unruly gray hair tamed, the old guy looked downright handsome.

"Hey Alex," he said with his slow smile. "How you holdin' up?"

"Hey Walt. Sounds like the whole world is up there. I'm okay other than that."

"Yeah, they sure are packing in. Been a long time since we had something as happy as a wedding. Everyone wants to pay their respects and wish the two of you best of luck."

"I'm going to need it to remember what I'm supposed to say."

Walt laughed, a huge, booming guffaw that brought a smile to Alex's face. That movement of his tense muscles felt fantastic.

"If I recall how these things generally work, Father Price will help you get through that part just fine."

He joined Alex in the next loop. Down one side of the row of gray steel support posts, up to the table against the far wall already bulging with an alarming amount of food. Then back down the other side toward the stairs Alex hoped he wouldn't be too nervous to climb when the time came.

"I sure would like to meet your folks, Alex," Walt said. "Be sure to introduce me if you get a chance."

"Well, you've met the ones you're going to. That would be Connor and Laura. No one else is going to be here."

"I'm real sorry to hear that."

"Eh, thank you. I'm not surprised. This is sort of how these things go, you know?"

Walt put a big hand on Alex's shoulder to stop him from turning and heading back toward the food table.

"That's too bad," he said, nodding. "They're missing their fine son marrying another fine young man, two of the best I've ever known. I'll tell you something I'm glad you don't remember for yourself. When I was your age, a long damn time ago, some people got themselves tied up in knots about two men or two women marrying. Thank God that time passed."

Alex nodded, glad he'd missed that time as well.

"What I'm wanting to say to you is a lot of people back then had to find their own families. The ones they was born to fell away, lots of times for the better. I hope there's nothing that hard in your past with your folks, Alex. But all you got to do is go upstairs and see how many people showed up to wish you and Etan well. That's the best kind of family. The one you make for yourself."

The heat in Alex's stomach shifted up to his throat, threatening to spill over into tears. He grabbed Walt in a quick, back pounding hug.

"Thank you, Walt. That's exactly what I needed to hear just now. I couldn't imagine a better family myself."

Walt nodded once before he turned to head up the steps toward the sanctuary.

"It's all gonna work out for you two," he said. "I feel it. See you up there."

Alex heard the door upstairs open, then Walt talking to someone before polished black shoes descended toward him. Connor Griffith leaned his head down, pretending to sneak.

"Everything all right down here?"

"Everyone's worried about me, huh?" Alex said with a laugh. "I'm not about to make a run for it, Connor. Not without your son."

"I'm awful glad to hear that." He carried two tiny green velvet boxes in his hand. "Just got these back, sorry they're so late."

"I don't know what you have there, so no need to apologize."

Etan's father flipped both boxes open before holding them out for Alex to see. Each held a silvery band with matching angular patterns.

"I know you two weren't planning on having rings," he said. "But I get the feeling you would have if we could get things like that anymore. Old Charlie Kennedy used to be the jeweler in town up until about ten years ago. He still does work on the side if you ask him nicely."

"Where did these come from?" Alex reached for the larger ring, but Connor moved that box aside.

"No, not yet. You take Etan's." He handed the box with the smaller ring to Alex. "These were my Mom and Dad's. Charlie melted them down together, then made these for you. You might remember Laura getting your ring size a couple of weeks ago?"

Alex grinned, not even trying to stop the tears now. Laura had brought out an ancient rattling key ring full of bunches of smaller rings while Alex was mostly distracted with the fitting for his suit. He'd accepted her tales of wanting to imagine what it would be like if only they could find something in time without a second thought.

Alex slipped the ring onto his pinky and turned it toward the overhead lights. The white gold gleamed, facets reflecting the light in patterns he'd been waiting his whole life to see.

"These are beautiful, Connor. I don't know what to say."

"Hope you'll forgive me for the biggest cliché on the face of the earth," Etan's father said, already heading up the steps. "But the words you're looking for are *I do*. See you in a couple of minutes."

Alex replaced the ring and dropped the box into his jacket pocket, wiping his eyes. He'd made a foolish promise to himself to keep it together until after the ceremony, one he was clearly going to break. That was by far the least important promise the day would bring.

Three minutes.

He adjusted the suit and ran his hands over his hair and beard, wishing he had a mirror down here for a last check. One more deep breath, and Alex walked up to join his true family.

Chapter 25

Etan sat with his eyes closed, listening to his heart beating. This meditation room beside the sanctuary was lined with acoustic pads that looked like giant gray egg cartons and a thick carpet that matched. All of that lead to near silence, broken only by that slow, regular beat.

He knew people were gathering just on the other side of the heavy oak door. More people than he'd expected despite his mother's warnings.

He and Alex had given up early on when it came to most of the plans for the day. His mother, her friends, even his father focused on their wedding to the exclusion of just about everything else in the world.

He certainly couldn't blame them for that. Even with what Alex had been telling him of his dreams, none of the news was good. This winter promised to bring the hunger everyone feared a year ago, with more crop failures from already weakened pollinators.

Trade was down to nearly non-existent, with fears of starvation along with fear of the various diseases. Not that anywhere on earth seemed to have surplus, not on a large scale. Wolf Branch still did.

Neither Etan, Alex, nor anyone else had forgotten their visitors from Maple Ridge.

He opened his eyes and got to his feet. An odd mirror arrangement that reflected itself endlessly, one on each opposite wall, worked well enough for him to make sure he looked as calm as he felt. Everything, from his suit to his shoes to the cufflinks he'd borrowed from his father, matched what he'd seen in his waking and sleeping dreams of this day.

The only thing missing was the ring.

The huge door opened, and his mother walked in with a burst of murmuring crowd noise. She was happier than Etan had seen her in a long time, glowing and gorgeous in her dark purple dress. He was relieved all over again that she'd taken on so much of the planning. For her sake, and for Alex's and his.

"Almost time," she said, hugging him. "Quite a crowd out there."

"You got your big wedding after all, Mom."

"I surely did, and I deserve it every bit as much as you do." She held out a small green box. "Your father and I wanted to give you these together, but Charlie just got here with them. Alex already has yours."

"Charlie? The jeweler?"

Etan opened the box and saw the one thing missing from the images in his mind. A white gold ring, too large for his own finger. He didn't have to ask Alex how much he'd love the geometric, angular patterns that caught the light almost like a gemstone.

"These came from your grandparents, Etan. Charlie melted them down together and made them for you."

He slipped the ring over his thumb.

"This is gorgeous, Mom. Thank you so much. I know Gemaw and Grampa would have been pleased."

"Of course they would have. They left it in their wills and final wishes, hon. Just like the house. One of those odd little paragraphs, make sure Etan has this if he needs it."

Etan smiled as the last piece of his wedding day slipped into place. Anne and Evan were with him after all.

"Did they leave me any other surprises?"

Laura Griffith shook her head, then reached up to adjust his tie.

"Nothing I'm going to tell you about until the time comes. I'm sure you won't be surprised Anne was clear about that, too."

"Not the least bit surprised. Almost time, isn't it?"

"Only a couple of minutes left. Father Price is already out there. Ready for all of this, son? You nervous?"

"I thought I would be, but I'm not. Not even a little bit. This just feels like the next step on the path we started years ago." Etan chuckled, shaking his head. "At a college party in the middle of a damn blizzard."

"Wherever it started, I'm so glad that path brought you both back home to us," she said, squeezing his hand. "See you at the reception."

Etan stood with his hand on the door, giving her time to get settled. His body felt like those mirrors, with a thousand reflections of himself slowly lining up. Focusing in on the next steps of his life, with Alex by his side.

When all the parts inside of Etan moved into the right place, he opened the door to see his love opening the one opposite the low stage.

True to his word, Father Price had removed all of the religious symbols. He stood in the middle in a black suit much like the ones the grooms wore. More candles than Etan had ever seen brought a perfect glow to the flowers, dried and fresh from the greenhouse, surrounding the spot left for the two of them.

He walked forward, unaware of the crowd, the music playing, the scent of all those flowers and candles. Etan only saw Alex, even more handsome in his wedding suit than he'd been walking out of the snow in Chicago.

And he saw him with traces of gray in his beard, the same silvery highlights gradually taking over his gorgeous red curls. Alex with metal-framed reading glasses, lines from countless smiles around his eyes.

They met in front of Father Price, Alex holding out his hand.

Young and strong and firm, old and worn and thin, with the ring he didn't yet have still on his third finger. Etan took his hand, and he saw his own many years from now, the veins and tendons visible just as they had been in his grandfather's right before he passed.

His fingers linked through his husband's, always.

Etan's composure held true almost until the end. Neither of them had expected it to mean much, not after several years together. Not with most of that time being consumed by planning for the end of everything rather than for new beginnings.

It was the simplest words that did it. Words that sounded so meaningless and unimportant when Father Price showed them his revised version.

What love has joined together, let nothing tear asunder.

Saying the same things to each other, with their whole worlds watching, granted their lives together a permanence they'd never had. A solidity, a foundation they could build from and depend on. They and everyone around them would come to depend on that bedrock in the months and years to come.

That was the last happy day anyone in Wolf Branch had for a long time.

Chapter 26

THE WHISPERS DRAGGED Alex out of an exhausted sleep, far deeper than usual after the stress and excitement of his wedding day. He blinked until he could see his watch. Three twenty-one.

Etan was curled up against his chest, an arm around his waist. He squeezed hard enough to force Alex's breath out.

"It's in the house *in the house!*"

Alex jolted wide awake, heart pounding, ears humming with the strain of listening for the slightest sound. All he could hear was Etan's ragged breathing.

"What's in the house?"

"The record. The ledger of days to come. Find it, Alex. Time is so very short."

"You mean the computers? We've looked at those."

Etan shook his head against Alex's chest.

"A journal in his own hand, hidden in the house. Meant for your eye. No other."

"In whose hand? I don't know where to look, Etan."

"In *Evan's* hand. Etan must never see."

Even after so many years, countless dreams, knowing he often wasn't really talking to Etan in the middle of the night, the words made Alex uneasy as he said them.

"Tell me where it is. I promise I won't let Etan see."

Etan whispered again, too soft and fast for Alex to hear. He leaned closer, struggling to understand.

"Okay, shhhhh. Go back to sleep, sweetie," he finally said. He kissed his husband, trying to stop the disturbing sound. "I'll find the journal. I'll go right now."

The frantic hissing slowed to even, regular breathing. Etan squeezed Alex tight, then turned over. The storm was over, at least inside his mind.

Alex was afraid it was only beginning for him.

He sat up, groping with his toes until he found his slippers, then grabbing his thick robe off the chair beside the door. The bedroom was cold enough with winter well underway. The rest of the house would be frigid with the fire long out. Grid power was too unreliable and expensive to run the furnace, and Alex hated to draw from their batteries for heat unless they had to.

He repeated what he'd caught of the whispers, feeling his way along the hall.

"In the library. Too high to see."

He flipped on the light, squinting in the glare. The room was almost exactly as it was the first day they'd stepped inside. According to Etan, it was just like his grandparents had left it. They'd created their own stacks of books on the end tables beside Anne and Evan's chairs, shifting and rearranging as they both searched for the clues that would help them survive the collapse.

Alex suspected it wouldn't be one huge secret revelation. Each small thing they learned and passed along to the community, to their family, would add up and give them the slim chance.

He scanned the top row of books, a collection of fiction that varied widely enough to seem like ten people had put them together. All were older than he, many older than his in-laws, all marked with wrinkles and creases of repeated reading.

Framed photos lined the highest shelf, many of them tucked right against the low ceiling. Anne and Evan, their parents, Connor and Laura. Etan at every possible awkward stage. Despite Alex's growing sense of urgency, his need to find this thing Etan so badly wanted him to have, he smiled at Anne's brown hair and green eyes. So much like his new husband.

Too high to see.

He grabbed the flashlight on the table between the two reading chairs. Etan had always insisted on having one in every room, by every door. The unreliable electricity had turned his desire into nearly an obsession.

Alex carried Anne's step ladder from the kitchen and held the wall as he slowly climbed up, not sure the delicate thing would hold him. Once he had both feet in place, it felt sturdy enough. He moved the light along the wall behind the photos. Nothing but an appalling layer of dust he wished he hadn't seen.

Except…

A glint of metal in the corner. Two hinges and a latch. A thick frame just above, the same as the door frames in the rest of the house.

He frowned, thinking what was on the other side of that wall. More books and photos in a recessed shelf built into the hallway. Evan Griffith had found an unused doorway to hide his journal. A man after Alex's own tinkering heart.

He moved the ladder and climbed up again. The photo in front of the rectangular opening was of Etan and his grandparents, their heads on either side of his, all of them smiling. Etan looking gawky and shy and adorable to Alex's eyes. Anne and Evan silver-haired and wrinkled, easily in their seventies or eighties. That must have been taken not long before they'd passed away.

Alex moved the frame aside, leaving tracks in the thick dust. He doubted anyone had opened this since the two of them had died, or not long after. The latch was a little stiff under his fingers, and the hinges protested movement after so much time.

He paused, listening. The house was still silent.

A small spiral-bound notebook with what looked like a faded red vinyl cover waited inside. The kind he'd seen in a few of his professor's offices in college, but he'd never used himself. Alex thought they'd stopped making them before he was born.

He stood on his tiptoes and pulled it out. The cover felt brittle, the wire around the left side rusty.

Dust floated through the flashlight beam as Alex climbed back down, shaking his head at this odd time capsule. If he'd needed more proof that Etan's dreams carried real weight and authority, this was too clear and strange to ignore.

Three yellowed envelopes slipped out of the notebook before he sat in Evan's chair. *Connor* and *Etan* were written in Evan's neat script on the front of two of them.

Alex's heart skipped when he saw his own name on the third. His fingers shook when he opened it.

Alex. We so wish we'd had a chance to meet you and get to know the wonderful man who will make our grandson so happy. It breaks my heart to introduce myself in such a way, and with such dreadful words inside this journal. We've only passed along what we had to. Please know Anne's seen you many times in her dreams. You and Etan have a chance to be as happy as we've been. We truly hope you take it. Much love, Evan Griffith.

Goosebumps raced over his already chilled flesh. That was exactly the same handwriting he'd seen on so many academic papers and books all over this room. Alex couldn't imagine anyone going to such lengths to create an elaborate hoax, complete with antique props and heavy gray dust.

Evan had to have written this at least three years before Alex met Etan.

And Etan dreamed of this, just as Anne had apparently dreamed of Alex.

He sat back in Evan's chair and pulled Anne's fluffy pink blanket up to his chest. He put Connor's envelope and his own back in the pocket inside the journal, leaving Etan's aside to give to him later. Easy enough to say it was tucked into one of the other books after he hid the journal again, before Etan woke.

Alex started to read.

$\sim$

THREE HOURS LATER, he stood on stiff and aching legs to start the wood stove before Etan woke up. Alex knew his shivering wasn't entirely from the cold, but he had to move. Do something. He hid the journal and put the step ladder away first.

The clouds were pink and red, the sun still hidden behind the mountain, when he stepped outside to get wood from the massive pile under the eaves. He glanced toward Connor and Laura's house several times before he went back inside.

The sacrifice will be terrible, but it will not be in vain. The sacrifice is necessary for any of you to survive.

"I should just burn the damn thing right now," he said under his breath as the kindling caught. "Forget about every fucking word."

Alex stared into the fire, wishing it would burn the words out of his mind. Out of his perfect little memory that he'd wished would fail him more than once in the middle of the night with Etan's dreams.

This was the first time he'd seen something so awful fully awake, and with his own eyes.

He added three heavy oak logs across the smaller ones and closed the door with its squeak he'd already come to love.

Maybe the whole journal was outdated now, fallen away into other choices and decisions. Etan said his grandmother often saw choices in her dreams and visions, though he never seemed to. Alex hoped something they'd already done, some action they'd unknowingly put into motion, would cancel out the horrible loss the journal warned him about.

Etan removed all of Alex's room for doubt when he started dreaming about Connor's sacrifice that night.

Chapter 27

ALEX LET his breath out slowly through his chilled lips, the stillness in his body steadying the gun. His feet were shoulder-width on the frosty ground behind their house, arms straight in front of him. He and Etan's father were much further back from the target on a bale of hay against the hillside than a couple of months ago, easily fifty feet instead of ten.

He squeezed the trigger, letting the revolver's momentum carry it upward, then sighting the target again. Sharp, metallic gunpowder smoke filled his nose with every deep breath.

Four shots rang out. Five. Six.

Even at this distance, Alex saw every bullet strike within an inch of the bright red bull's-eye. His new father-in-law clapped him on the back, and he heard Connor's laughter through the earmuffs.

"Damn, son. I believe you're a better shot than I am now!"

"Hardly," Alex said, the frigid air digging into his ears when he pulled the earmuffs off. "I'm a hell of a lot better than I used to be."

Alex holstered the revolver as they walked toward the target to verify the accuracy they'd both seen. His right wrist and palm ached from the repeated recoil. He wanted to practice a bit more with the semi-automatic pistol on his left hip before his hands got too cold, but he couldn't pretend that was the only reason they were out here.

"You handle a gun as well as Etan does," Connor said. "Once you put your mind to it, you're a natural."

"He'd never admit it. At least not where I can hear him."

Every bullet hole was within the smallest ring. Connor pulled it down and handed it to Alex, beaming. He pushed another one over the sharp sticks driven into the hay.

"Keep this in case he gives you trouble about being a better shot than you."

"Will do."

Connor picked up his dark green metal Thermos on the picnic table near the house, taking away Alex's chance to distract both of them with the next practice round. He poured steaming light brown coffee into two metal coffee cups. Alex sipped his, staring at the narrow valley beyond the small back yard. He was prepared for Connor's overly sweet concoction after nearly two years.

He wasn't prepared for his father-in-law's next words.

"You're up awfully early for just a couple days after your wedding. What's on your mind, Alex?"

Connor was watching him, one eyebrow raised, but he was smiling. That expression was so much like Etan's that Alex laughed.

"Etan had to go into town to help out at the cannery. Not much time for a honeymoon these days. What gives you the idea I've got something on my mind?"

"Just a feeling, I guess. You're way too good at shooting to need an old man's help any more. I figure you have something you want to talk about without your husband along. Or my wife."

"You got me," Alex said. He was out of time. He pulled his black gloves on and sat beside Connor on the picnic table, feet up on the bench. "I've been reading Evan's journal, the one hidden behind the bookcase. Ever flip through it?"

Connor held the cup in both hands, breathing in the steam before he took another drink.

"I have. I think it was meant for you a lot more than me, but I read through the whole thing. I imagine you found a few things he wrote about me that you don't like."

"That's an understatement." Alex chewed his bottom lip, part of his mind still trying to find a way to avoid this conversation. Even more, he was desperate to stop the things Evan wrote about. "How the hell did you find it? I didn't have a clue that door was there until Etan dreamed about it."

"Dad left me a note for after he passed. You should have found it, right there in the front."

"I didn't read it," Alex said. "It was meant for you."

"Well, you're the one other person on earth who needs to read it. I want you to. He just said that notebook was for me and my future son-in-law." He grinned at Alex. "Dad grew up in a different time. Guess he thought I needed a warning that Etan was going to be so happy. He did leave me a real warning, though, that Etan should never read that journal. Or anyone else in the family. It was meant for me, and for you."

"Does Laura know what he wrote?"

"No. And I don't want her to. Does Etan?"

"If he does, he hasn't said anything to me. I'm damn sure he would have if he knew you were supposed to be some kind of sacrifice."

Connor nodded.

"I'm sure he would, too. Laura would string me up if she saw it." He turned to Alex, his green eyes clear and steady. "You know the end game, son. Etan dreams about it. Dad wrote it, and Mom dreamed it over and over again. Neither one of them ever said a word to me, but they made sure to write it all down. Every single thing in that journal was sent to us for a good reason."

"I need to know if there's any way to avoid this, Connor. Please just tell me the truth."

The older man refilled both their cups, blowing on his own before taking a sip. Alex was afraid he wasn't going to answer. He knew he wouldn't have the courage to ask again.

"You read the same thing I did," Connor finally said. "I don't know what it's going to be any more than you do, or when."

"Did Evan talk to you about it? Or Anne? They talked to Etan about a lot of things they never wrote down."

"And there's a lot more they wrote down and didn't tell him

about," Connor said, his hand on Alex's shoulder. "This is a hard thing for you to know about on your own, but Etan carries so much in his mind already. Dad talked to me about Mom's dreams. How talking to him helped her get back to sleep, but *he* sometimes couldn't. They both knew Etan would find you, Alex. I hope you get back to sleep eventually."

"Not lately I don't. Listen, I get the feeling Sandy knows where a group of scientists are hiding, close to Chicago. If we explain what's going on, we can get you up there and away from this."

Connor shook his head again. He rubbed his bare hands together, then blew into them.

"Is Etan dreaming about it? What's going to happen to me?"

Alex leaned forward with his elbows on his knees, rubbing his hair. The black fabric gloves rasped in his ears.

"He started dreaming about it night before last, right after he told me exactly where to find Evan's journal. He's not seeing when or how either. He doesn't remember it when he wakes up, but he's sobbing in his sleep, every time. I *can't* pretend I don't know."

"Is he saying we need to stop this, Alex? Whatever's coming? Or does he just see it, like Mom did?"

"I don't care about that!" Alex slammed his fists into his own thighs, his tired right wrist protesting.

Distant shots cut through the cold air a few minutes later, breaking the long silence between the two men. Someone else out practicing. Probably for the same reasons.

Getting ready for the end of the world.

"He only ever sees something is going to happen to you," Alex said. "He's never said a word about stopping it."

"Same as Mom did, then. Did you know she remembered her dreams? Pretty much every one of them, even before she started telling them to Dad?"

"Yeah, Etan told me about that. He thinks that's why she had so much trouble, that he stays sane as he is because he rarely remembers. After hearing what he sees, I believe it."

"Well, think about that," Connor said. "She knew this was going to happen to me. So did Dad. She either never saw what the sacrifice will be, or she and Dad decided not to write it down for some reason. But they both knew I was going to die. I know you want to have a family someday, son. Raise your own children. Do you really think they would have made this choice if they didn't have a damn good reason?"

"It is a fucking curse," Alex whispered.

"Mom never thought so, at least not that she admitted to me. She understood it was part of what led to being with Dad, and having me, and later Laura and me having Etan. Think you would have met him if it weren't for his curse?"

Alex glanced at Connor, then shook his head. He didn't say what he was thinking for a change. If it weren't for his own curse, none of this would have been part of his life.

Not Chicago. Not Etan. Not this morning in the early Virginia winter, talking to the father he'd wished he had his whole life.

The father he was about to lose.

"This is going to break Etan's heart. Mine, too."

"I don't have to ask if you read to the end of the journal. You're not the type who can stand not knowing something. That's part of what makes this so tough. Whatever's going to happen to me will let Etan's heart keep beating, and yours. Everything else depends on that."

Alex crossed his arms across his stomach, trying to stop the shivering deep inside from spreading to his whole body. Every word Connor said was in Evan's journal, and in Etan's dreams, night after night. For the first time in his life, Alex wished he didn't know what was coming toward them.

"How am I supposed to live with this?" he said. "I can never tell Etan I knew. Not as long as I live."

"Same way I live with not telling Laura. Or Etan. Same way my parents lived with not telling me. I put it out of my mind as much as I possibly can and enjoy the time I have with my family. They'll both make it through to the other side of whatever this thing is. So will you. That has to be enough for both of us."

"You're a stronger man than I am."

"No, I'm not. You witness these terrible dreams and remember them when Etan can't. I never have. You're the man who's strong enough to make it through and help him make it through. And you're the man who's going to help raise my grandbabies, Alex. You'll be a fantastic father."

Alex squeezed his eyes closed, but hot tears ran down his cheeks anyway. Not because of his father-in-law's words, though they were bad enough.

He'd felt and seen the motion, in the wispy clouds in the dark blue sky, the bare trees swaying in the wind. His condemnation flowed from the direction of frost-killed grass on the ground all around them.

Even when he had no choices, Alex was certain he was making the wrong ones.

"If I'm half the father you are, Connor, our kids will be just fine."

Chapter 28

ALEX SAT in Evan's chair, pretending to read one of his fiction books while Etan read one of Anne's. He couldn't tell if his husband was making progress on the story or not. Alex hadn't turned a page in at least half an hour. He kept glancing toward that hidden compartment behind the bookcase.

He was equally tempted to either take the notebook to the wood stove after all or to hand it to Etan and watch him read every word.

The phone rang in the living room, a harsh, churning old-fashioned ring. Alex usually found that a charming feature of the heavy old black phone they'd found in the basement, one that worked during the more frequent power outages. Mobile phones had never gotten much signal at their house even before so many things started to erode.

Tonight the sound of that ring drilled deep into his skull, twisting and echoing and building on itself.

His teeth seemed to vibrate with it. His bones.

Whatever was coming toward them would get well and truly underway with whatever Etan heard on the other side of that phone.

Alex closed his eyes, trying to hear half of the conversation he dreaded knowing more about. He couldn't make out a word, not until Etan stepped back into the library. He was pale and his hand shook when he reached for Alex's.

"We need to go down to Mom and Dad's."

"Connor?" Alex said before he had a chance to think.

"No, they're both fine. Everything out in the world just got worse. One hell of a lot worse. They're still getting a couple of news channels."

"Anything they can't tell us about?" he said.

Please. Just let us stay here, safe and warm and ignorant for one more night.

I don't want to know any more.

I *can't*.

"Dad said we need to see it," Etan said. "Some kind of disease in the corn, way more serious than what we've seen before. This may be what makes it all crash."

"The corn everyone here has been planting less and less of, without either of us having to say a word about what Evan wrote." Alex stood beside Etan with his arm around him. "We can go whenever you're ready."

"I'm not. I don't even want to be. But if we wait five minutes, I might not ever go out the door again."

CONNOR AND LAURA were as pale as Etan, and Alex knew he probably looked worse. On their television, the headline screamed white against a blood-red background.

WORLDWIDE PANDEMIC AND STARVATION: FATALITIES MOUNT.

"They're saying it's in feed corn, and all the animals that eat it." Laura held out her hand, and Alex sat beside her on the couch. Etan sat beside his father. "Everything they make out of corn, too. Soda, syrup, plastic. All kinds of food. Even baby formula. Some kind of fungus, getting shipped all around the world for a long time. They're saying that awful stomach flu that's been killing so many people and animals was really this thing called aflatoxin."

"They test for everything now," Etan said, his voice shaky. "How could they miss something that kills people?"

"They *did* test for this," Connor said. "Big farmers have for decades. They used to catch the fungus before corn or anything else got into the food supply. But it mutated or changed, or someone changed it on purpose. Weaponized it. Now the toxin doesn't show up until it's way too late. Mom dreamed about poison in the air and water. Dad wrote about the risks of disease in giant fields full of the same crop."

Alex spoke out loud without meaning to, his reeling mind losing control over his mouth.

"Etan dreams about the same thing."

He tried not to, but he finally turned toward his father-in-law. Connor didn't seem angry or afraid, things Alex felt more than anything else right now. He looked curious. Wondering if Alex was going to keep their secret.

In that second, Alex had no idea whether he'd manage or not.

"There were riots all over the world last winter," Etan said. "With so many people knowing they'll get sick and it could have been prevented, this year is going to be worse."

"No one in the mountains has gotten much food in from outside for months now," Alex said, trying to shake fear for Connor from his mind and heart. "Turns out that's a good thing, but shortages are already bad in other towns. Too many people know Wolf Branch has more than we need."

"We have several people armed and well-trained," Connor said. "You and Alex are two of the best. We may need to set up guards at the food bank and cannery."

"That's not going to be enough," Laura said, squeezing Alex's hand in her chilly fingers. "So many people have stores at their houses. We all do. Protecting all of that's going to be impossible."

"Etan dreamed of everyone living in town," Alex said. He was surprised his voice still worked. "Neither of us could figure out why, since that makes water and sewer and everything else harder to maintain. This could be the reason."

The phone rang, another noisy old model that made everyone

jump. The scene on the TV screen shifted as Connor answered. Now a giant white LIVE took up the left corner, and no one needed the banner running underneath.

That word Laura used, *aflatoxin*. And video of a riot. Not in a poor country on the other side of the planet this time.

Philadelphia.

The screen split, adding horrible, violent scenes from San Diego.

"That was Harry Mullins," Etan's father said, standing in the doorway. "They've already got a few people staying at the cannery tonight. We'll get together in the morning and work out a schedule."

He stared into Alex's eyes again. Alex wondered, not for the first time, how much of Anne's talent Connor had inherited after all.

"Feels like we have to get this next part right," Etan said. "What we do here is going to put a bunch more things into motion. I can't even imagine where all that will end up."

"Let's try to get all the main people involved as soon as we can," Alex said. "Make sure we aren't working against each other."

He didn't say what he was feeling.

If all of them were together, maybe whatever was supposed to hit Connor would hit someone else. He struggled to block the other families out of his mind.

He wasn't proud, or trying to be stubborn.

Alex simply couldn't stand his own family being torn apart so soon after he'd finally found them.

Chapter 29

The exhaustion of his own fear, and of not being able to sleep every time Etan spoke of Connor's death in the darkness, caught up with Alex when they got back home that night. His sleep was deep and dreamless.

Etan's words, clear as if he were wide awake, yanked Alex into consciousness a few hours later.

"The time has come. What we do now decides the future."

Etan was facing away from him, close up against his body. He fought a nearly overpowering urge to shake Etan, turn on the bright overhead light, scream at him to stop. He touched his shoulder instead.

"The time for what, sweetie?"

"So many sacrifices, so much loss. All to prepare for this moment. Greater sacrifices will see us through or see us extinct."

Evan's words, and Etan's, of Anne seeing choices surged into Alex's mind. After her long life of options and free will, were they reduced to only one way forward?

"Do you see anything else we can do, Etan? Do we have choices? Decisions we can make?"

"Each choice has consequences. None easy to live with. Most impossible to live through."

"Tell me what our choices are," Alex said. Every cell in his body screamed this was foolhardy, the best way to make difficult nights intolerable, but he couldn't stop himself. "Maybe I can find another way."

Etan breathed deeply several times. Alex had time to wonder if it would be harder to never know what his lover would have said or to hear the words.

"Connor's sacrifice is the way forward," Etan said, tears obvious in his voice. "Every other way is disaster."

"This whole thing is disaster. Just tell me, please. I won't do the wrong thing. I promise."

"Mary's wish will see us overrun. Starvation and torture. Those who destroy us will die in their own turn. All the lights of humanity will go out."

"I understand," Alex said. "I won't let that happen."

"The task is far harder than you believe. Her words are strong, her followers many. Without the sacrifice, she will triumph. All will be lost."

"There must be another way. Another sacrifice." Alex gritted his teeth against the nausea working from his stomach through his whole body. If he couldn't say this, how could he possibly let it happen? "Someone besides…besides Connor."

Etan shook his head.

"Only one other would drag us away from Mary's madness. The loss too great. The end merely postponed. The darkness unavoidable."

Alex pulled Etan's shoulder, gently turning him onto his back. He needed to see his face, even in the faint light. All the nerves and blood in his body thrummed in time, anticipating the horrible words his husband would speak.

"One or the other," Etan said, his head turning his sightless eyes toward Alex's face. "A beloved man cut down for all to see and bring everyone into alignment. Toward a broken future."

Alex put his hand over Etan's mouth, shaking his own head.

Too much.

Etan was right, as Evan and Connor had been before him. Alex wouldn't be able to live with any of these choices.

Etan's lips moved under his fingers. The shape of the names was enough even without the sound.

Etan, or Alex himself.

"Why?" Alex whispered, removing his hand. "Will no one else do?"

"No one else can end the madness. Mary brings us all to quick ruin. The loss of Alex or Etan prolongs the suffering to no end. The loss of Connor gives all a chance to survive."

"I can't. I can't do this."

"The paths are clear before you now. The choice yours alone to make."

Alex turned away from Etan and curled up as tight as he could. No matter what he did, even if he left Wolf Branch right now and never looked back, he would never be free of this decision. He was afraid he'd never be able to smile, sleep, breathe again.

Etan sighed, his mind and body released from the dream. He curled against Alex's back and legs.

The warmth never made it through to Alex's heart.

Chapter 30

Etan brushed eraser debris from his spreadsheet yet again, keeping his eyes focused on the increasingly messy schedule. Starting with everyone marking up their own printed copy, same as they'd always done, seemed to make sense an hour ago rather than worrying about getting copies made afterward.

That was before Alex got himself into some kind of fucking auto-dispute mode neither Etan, Alex himself, nor anyone else could break him out of.

Six others gathered around Linda's conference table in her office at the high school, trying to agree on a work schedule for the next few weeks. These get-togethers never had been long enough or formal enough to call them meetings.

Just like the disastrous mess at the auditorium, a friendly few minutes had somehow stretched into a grueling marathon. The afternoon sun faded perilously close to early evening through the high windows along one wall, glinting through Alex's red hair and beard.

His odd resistance to adding the patrol schedule for guarding their supplies had them all tense enough that Etan wasn't the only one glaring at his husband. He felt less and less like protecting Alex from everyone else's frustration with every passing second, every objection.

These two people shouldn't patrol together. This area needed three guards instead of two. One instead of three. Alex pushed the tiniest details into endless discussion.

Etan's gaze was drawn to the huge map of the world behind Linda's ancient, scarred wooden desk. His mind filled in the growing problems in cities and countries in a blink of his eyes. Riots now in every wealthy nation to go along with all-out war in most of the poor ones.

Cities all over the US falling into chaos one after another, seemingly a new one every hour. The closest so far was Cincinnati, only a few hours away.

His imagination, or maybe his waking nightmare, saw each of those cities as a glowing dot. The centers of human population all over the world.

The death count from riots and violence was estimated to be well into the millions in the US alone. The oncoming winter was expected to kill far more with starvation and the horrible foodborne disease, if people didn't manage the trick themselves first.

The lights on the map of the world winked out in Etan's mind, one after the other. He looked away, too afraid to see how many would be left in the end.

Wolf Branch's good luck couldn't possibly hold out much longer, not with the way he and everyone else were feeling. That surely explained some of Alex's attack of peevishness, but Etan hadn't had any dreams for days.

Those two things, Alex's distress and Etan's sound sleep, didn't match up.

"I'm not sure what else we can do to make this work out," Linda said, rubbing her eyes. Her right pinky was smudged gray from the pencil she'd been writing with. "No one seems to be happy no matter what we do."

"I think we need to take a little bit of a break," Etan's father said. He glanced at Etan, then met Alex's gaze across the table. "We're getting all bent out of shape over this and chasing our tails."

"Sure," Etan said, shoving his chair back with a grinding noise he immediately regretted. "Walk with me, Alex?"

Alex stared at him, and the hot anger in Etan's chest cooled in an instant. Alex didn't look mad or stubborn, nothing like the way he was acting. He looked nervous and scared half to death.

"I think I'm going to head over to the cannery, get something for all of us to drink," Etan's father said. "You have the key, Alex?"

Now Etan was watching his father, more confused than annoyed by his strange behavior. That sounded more like an invitation than a simple request for a key.

"Sure, Connor," Alex said. He slid the key across the table, avoiding meeting the older man's eyes. "I'll be back in a few."

Alex walked out of the room alone without looking back.

Father Price scowled at the open door. Etan couldn't remember ever seeing him so frustrated.

"Any idea what's got him so ornery, Etan? I've never known Alex to argue every little thing like this."

Etan shook his head, then stood, not sure whether he should follow Alex or give him that time to himself. He hated to even think such a thing, but he hoped Alex decided to skip the rest of this meeting altogether.

"I have an idea," Etan's father said. He was scooting the key around on the table, making an irritating scratching noise, but he made no move to leave the room. "Let's go with the work schedule from last month. Whoever's not on at the food bank or the cannery can fill in on patrol where the new volunteers can't. I think that will leave one of us on just about every shift, won't it?"

"It would," Linda said, flipping through her folder to the older schedule. "What makes you think he won't argue about that, too? Sorry, Etan."

"No, don't apologize," Etan said. "I don't know what's going on with him either. Maybe he'll see a pattern that worked several times before, and he'll feel better about the whole thing."

Etan rubbed at his temples, trying to stop an alarm blaring through his head.

Patterns. Alex saw patterns better than any of them, and his behavior had been following an ever growing pattern of upset and distress for several days now. Ever since, well, a few days after their wedding.

Frustrated as he was, Etan couldn't get himself worked up over imagined regrets on his new husband's part. He'd stood beside Alex that day. There was no mistaking the look in his eyes, the sound of his voice. The heat of their lovemaking that night.

Something else was going on here, and not just with Alex.

"Yeah, let's go with that old schedule," he said. "I'd love some of the cherry cider, Dad. Alex could definitely use a beer."

"What? Sure, of course. I'll be back in a minute."

Etan's internal dislocation increased as his father walked out, shaking his head. Without asking what anyone else wanted. He hadn't remembered offering to get drinks at all. That had all been a ploy to get Alex to go with him.

Now Etan had to get the truth out of both of them, unless what they were hiding matched up. He had an unsettling feeling it did.

"Does everyone have a copy of this old schedule?" Linda said, pushing hers toward the middle of the table. "We can use these blank ones to do the patrol schedule and hopefully be done with it."

"We're done with it now," Alex said. No one had noticed him standing in the doorway. "That's fine, Linda. We can use that this month and see what happens. We'll adjust to whatever comes, like we always have."

He put his hand on Etan's shoulder as he walked by. Etan grabbed it and looked up. Alex started to turn away, then closed his eyes. When he met Etan's gaze, his blue eyes were red around the edges.

"You okay?" Etan whispered. He kissed Alex's hand where his ring finger joined his palm.

"I'm as okay as I'm going to be for a while," he said. He sat, linking his fingers through Etan's. "This isn't going to be easy, Etan. Whether anyone comes here causing trouble or not, we're about to witness the end of the world."

"Yeah, we are," Etan's father said as he walked in. "Nothing's ever going to be the same again. We'll get through it the best we can as long as we watch out for each other."

Alex watched his father-in-law arrange several bottles of their cider and beer, sweat already beading on the pale brown glass. He stared up at Connor with an intensity that only made Etan more uncomfortable.

"Thanks, Connor," Alex said, taking a beer and a cherry cider. "You too, Linda. I'm sorry for being such an asshole. Let's get this wrapped up and get out of here."

Linda put a chipped white coffee mug in front of each of them. Not the most appropriate glassware in the world, perhaps, but more than adequate for such a tough day.

"No one's happy about this, Alex," she said. She added a few threadbare white towels to the middle of the table. "You're doing the best you can, just like the rest of us."

Etan's father must have carried the bottles as carefully as any bartender in an elegant restaurant back in the city. Not one overflowed when they flipped the tops back.

"To doing the best we can," Etan said, holding up his mug. The bubbles in the light red liquid landed on his wrist.

"And living through the end of the world," Alex said.

Etan couldn't help but notice how much those words sounded like a threat rather than a promise. He was afraid that was exactly what they'd turn out to be.

Chapter 31

ALEX WAS thankful for the silence on the drive home after they picked Laura up from the food pantry in town. He knew his mother-in-law was perfectly capable of handling her own handgun, probably a bit better than any of the men in her family as it turned out.

He was still relieved an armed guard was always there any time the food pantry was open. That wouldn't likely protect Connor when the time came, but at least Etan wouldn't lose both parents.

Laura didn't even try to lighten the mood in the vehicle after greeting the three of them. She picked up on the tension as fast as she usually did.

That made Alex as guilty as anything else about the future intruding so horribly on their present. She couldn't have that many more conversations left with her husband, and his own pissy little temper tantrum had stolen at least one of them.

None of them spoke until Connor parked in front of Alex and Etan's house.

"Any reason we should bother getting together for dinner tonight?" Laura said, turning around to look at them.

"I don't know if any of us are fit for company," Connor said. He rubbed her shoulder.

"Well, you're certainly not," she said. Alex was relieved she touched her husband's hand. "Maybe the three of you can take a nap or something. Or tell me what the hell the problem is."

"We'll see what we can do," Etan said. "Talk to you later."

Alex walked toward the house, glancing back over his shoulder even though every nerve in his body told him not to. Connor watched him, nodded once, then turned the car around and left.

"What's it going to be, Alex?" Etan stood with one foot on the porch steps, staring after the car. "You going to tell me what's up or make me ask my father?"

Alex crossed the yard, detouring around the flower and vegetable beds casting long shadows in the twilight, wondering how long his mind could possibly stay so utterly jumbled and useless. Hundreds of words flashed through his brain, every one too fast to make it all the way to his mouth. He put his hand over Etan's on the wooden rail.

"I'm just tired, sweetie," he said. That much was the truth. "Maybe I do need that nap."

Etan shook his head, the movement small but impossible to ignore. The compression of his lips made Alex's heart plummet.

"Perfect, that's where we'll start. I'll brew us a pot of coffee, and we're going to sit down and have a talk we probably should have had a few days ago."

He went inside, letting the screen door slam behind him.

Alex wanted nothing more than to sink down on the concrete steps and stay right there. Pretend he was in front of their apartment in Chicago, or even in his parents' back yard in Wisconsin. Worried about things he couldn't even bring to mind now that the whole world had changed. Either place felt a hundred years ago and a million miles away.

And Etan was in neither one of them, and never would be again.

He pulled himself up the steps and went inside.

What he and Etan had read about the disease spreading all over the world—started by someone intentionally infecting huge corn crops—had them both avoiding their library. The fungus that spread the horrific toxin wasn't only in corn and things made from it anymore. Peanuts, walnuts, wheat, even cotton crops had been infected and spread the toxin to humans and animals.

Even if the world could afford to destroy so much food when millions were starving, it was too late for that in more places than Alex wanted to think about. The genetically altered fungus lingered in the soil itself. Liver failure, immune-system failure, cancer, and a dozen other problems awaited exposed people and animals who managed not to starve to death.

Alex couldn't think of a hell in any mythology or imagination deep and damned enough for whoever spread this poison.

Instead of the library, he waited on the couch in the living room. The same gray couch they'd brought with them, the first piece of decent furniture he'd bought for himself before he ever met Etan. He hoped they'd stored up enough good memories in the sturdy canvas to withstand this bad one.

Etan brought two steaming mugs in, the rich, sharp smell alone making Alex feel more alert. He handed one to Alex and sat at the opposite end of the couch. After a few minutes, Alex knew he needed to say something. He couldn't imagine what his husband was imagining for himself, and he didn't want to leave Etan in the kind of pit he could work himself down into.

But he had no way to bring this up, and no idea how he'd respond once Etan did.

"Great, so you're tired," Etan finally said. "That doesn't make a whole lot of sense to me, Alex. I haven't had any dreams for at least a week now, at least not that you've told me about. That's never happened before in all these years. Why would you be getting more and more tired, and acting more like a jerk, when you've been sleeping through the night beside me?"

Alex was afraid to drop his gaze and confirm Etan's suspicions that he'd been hiding something, and the pain and worry in his husband's eyes was tearing his heart out. It was probably way too late, but he at least had to try to protect Connor's secret.

"You've been dreaming the same thing for a while now," he said, glancing away when he took a sip of the strong coffee. "More about crops failing, especially the corn everyone's so dependent on. Nothing new to tell you about."

Etan nodded again, his lips disappearing into a thin, pale line.

"Did you know I can feel the click when you tell me about one of my dreams? A shift inside me, your words matching up with whatever happens inside my head?"

"No," Alex whispered. "You never told me that."

"I never had to before. You never lied to me about a dream. I didn't know how that would hit me until just this minute. That one felt like splinters inside my mind. You'll have to do better."

"That's the best I *can* do, Etan."

"Is my father going to lie to me, too, Alex? Does he know what this huge secret is that I've been dreaming about?"

Alex pressed the heels of his hands into his eyes, willing Etan not to make the leap to how many dreams he'd kept to himself before they left Chicago three years ago. Admitting to that, back before he'd had any idea the conversations in the middle of the night could affect more than the two of them, had been a hell of a lot easier than trying to dodge this particular bullet.

"The only thing I can tell you is this dream wasn't about you or me," he said, folding his hands in his lap. "It doesn't feel right to tell you."

"You act like you don't understand a fucking thing about me. Anything that upsets you and my father this much absolutely affects me. If you're not being honest with me about a dream this important, how can I believe what you've told me about all the others? We could have thrown our lives in Chicago away over some bit of bullshit you made up to see how far you could push me."

"You can't really believe that," Alex said, forcing the words out through a tight throat. "You *have* to know I'd never do that to you. You just said you feel it when I'm telling you the truth about the dreams."

"Yeah, I did say that," Etan said. "I didn't say anything about when you decide to hide them from me altogether. If I can't trust you, I can't ever know what's coming. If I can't trust you, there's no point in surviving."

Alex pulled his feet up on the couch and wrapped his arms around his knees. He still felt exposed in a million agonizing ways.

"There's no way I can do the right thing."

Etan moved beside Alex and put both arms around him

"You told me not to hide from you that same way, remember? When we first talked about these fucking dreams. If we can't trust each other, especially when it comes to this, we're lost, Alex. We're lost."

"I know that. I believe that. The thing is *you* keep saying you must never know," Alex said, his voice breaking along with his heart. "'Etan must never see.' Every time you have that dream, you make me promise. What the hell am I supposed to do?"

"You know it's too late for that, don't you? I can't live with not knowing, and you can't live with telling me. I've wondered before if this whole mess is something evil using us without having the grace to tell us why. Nothing else makes any sense."

"The only thing that makes any sense to me right now is you," Alex said. He kissed Etan, relieved when he responded to his touch instead of drawing away. Alex needed the contact more than he needed to breathe. "Hurting you like this doesn't. I'm trapped no matter which way I turn."

"We both are." Etan held his forehead against Alex's, then stroked his cheek and sat back. "This probably isn't fair to ask, but none of this is fair. You said I'm not supposed to see whatever the dreams are about. Is there something I *am* supposed to see?"

Alex groaned, covering his face with his hands. He should leave lying to people who were better at it.

"Yeah, there is," he said. He walked into the library and pulled the old envelope from the top shelf where he'd left it. "I forgot about this, but yeah. You're supposed to see it."

Etan flinched when he saw his name on the envelope.

"My grandfather's handwriting." He slipped his thumb under the seal. "You didn't read it?"

"No, E. It wasn't mine to read."

Alex sat beside Etan, watching his face. His lovely green eyes, wide and unbelieving at first, slowly filled with tears and closed. He held the note out for Alex to read.

My dearest Etan. We're terribly sorry such difficult times will be part of your life, but we're overjoyed you have Alex to help you through. What happens won't seem fair, now and in your future. You'll both deal with heartache and sorrow no one should have to, separately and together. The love you share and the lives you build out of the struggle will all be worth it in the end. Take care of each other, and never forget how much we love you. Grampa and Gemaw.

"Where did you find this?" Etan said, his voice soft. "They died three years before I met you."

"It was… You told me where to find it in your dreams."

"And there was something for you, too," Etan said. "Something I'm not supposed to see."

"Mine said they only passed along what they had to, and that we have a chance to be as happy as they were." He turned away, shaking his head. "A lot of the same things about difficult times ahead of us, too."

Etan drummed his fingers on Alex's knee, staring into space.

"I need to talk to my father. I won't tell him you said anything. You don't have to go if you don't want to. But I have to talk to him."

Relief so strong it hit like a marijuana buzz from his college years flooded through Alex. He'd done the best he could, now it was between Etan and Connor. That was the first thing he felt like he could live with for several days.

"I'll go, sweetie. I'll talk to your Mom so you can have time with your Dad. He doesn't want her to know, either."

"I'm glad it's not just me."

The phone rang, the awful, grinding buzz setting Alex's teeth and nerves and bones on edge again.

Just like the night the riots started.

"Etan, don't…"

But Etan answered, turning to stare at Alex after a few seconds.

His face was dead white.

Chapter 32

ETAN'S MIND REELED, threatening to take his body down with it. He didn't need Alex to speak the words to know the dream was moving into place all around him. That familiar deep alignment pulled all rational thought into the black abyss with his heart.

"Now. We have to go now, Alex."

Alex started to speak, then his face turned hard and cold.

"Those raiders. The ones from from the cannery."

"Maybe," Etan said, grabbing his holster from the table beside the door. "Probably. Whoever it is already hit the food pantry, soon as it got dark. Threw a firebomb in when they didn't find what they wanted. Only the one building burned before they got it out, but that distracted everyone. There's a damn blackout in town, of course, one they may have caused. No lights to see where they are."

"We have to stop Connor from going down there."

Alex slipped his own holster low over his hips, then added two leather bags with extra ammunition from hooks beside the door.

"That was Mom," Etan said, the spinning in his mind making him dizzy. "He left a few minutes ago, as soon as he got the first call."

Alex's face twisted, his lips drawing back from his teeth.

"Let me get the rifles. I don't know how to shoot the damn things yet, but someone else will."

Etan ran down the steps and out to his grandfather's car, dropping the keys twice when he tried to start it.

"Why the hell didn't you tell me, Evan?" he whispered. "We could have done something to stop this!"

Alex opened the back door, dropping three rifles and another ammunition bag. He slammed the door hard enough to rock the car on its springs.

"I think we need to stop and get your mother."

"I'm not dragging her into this mess. She's better off right where she is."

"Hang on, listen," Alex said. "She's the one who mentioned everyone having stores of food at home, remember? If this is a big raid, especially if they're local, they'll know that. We can take her to the sheriff's office or something, but I don't want to leave her out here alone."

"You don't know her as well as you think you do," Etan said. "If we take her into the middle of this, we'd have to lock her in the jail to keep her out of whatever's going on."

He drove as fast as he dared, watching the woods beside the gravel road. The idea of gangs roaming the mountains made too much sense to ignore. The sky still glowed with a faint purplish light, but the trees were in full darkness. He smelled Alex's sweat, and his own.

"I know you can't say any more than you have to," Etan said. "But could we have stopped this? Whatever's happening?"

"This may not be what you dreamed about. You never say exactly what happens, and Evan didn't either."

"I can feel it, Alex! The dream is all around us! Please, just answer me."

"All either of you said was there were choices, Etan. All of them are bad. Bad enough that stopping the dream isn't one of them."

"Bad for who? For my father? Are all of them bad for him?"

They turned onto the paved road, unlined and pure black. Only a minute or so until they were at his mother's house. Every second Alex waited drove the terror deeper into Etan's heart.

"They're all bad for him," Alex said. "And for us. The other choices… They end up with all the lights of humanity going out."

The sweat turned to ice on Etan's skin. He didn't try to stop himself from shouting.

"Did I say that to you before? About the lights? Alex? Did I?"

"No, not while you were awake," Alex said, frightened, nearly shouting himself. "Not until last night."

"Christ," Etan whispered. He turned up the driveway to his mother's house. "That's what my grandmother dreamed about when she was a kid. I told you about the library she was trapped in? She saw lights going out on a map of the world in there. Whole cities dying. One after another until only a few were left. Or if things were bad for her, before she was with my grandfather, all the lights went out. I saw the same thing at that meeting this afternoon on Linda's map."

"That's our other choice, E. Some survive, or everyone dies. That's what we're faced with."

The motion light in front of his parents' house was still on from his father leaving.

Everything, from the thick air in his lungs to the frost sparkling on the grass to the bruised light fading from the sky told Etan they were running out of time.

Chapter 33

Laura met them at the door, wearing her cold weather gear and handguns. She was about to follow Connor in her own car, whether he wanted her to or not. Alex was equal parts impressed with her determination and heartbroken that she was going into the middle of whatever storm awaited them.

His body felt overloaded, muscles and nerves twitching with excess energy. Only massive electrical storms coming in across the lake in his childhood or touring a huge power plant had ever hit Alex that way. He was half convinced blue sparks would fly off his fingers if he got close to metal.

"Do you know any more about what's happening?" Etan said when she got into the front seat.

"Only what Father Price said when he called," Laura said. "Whoever this is has at least a little bit of training, and they know where to look. They're scattered all over town, but no one doubts they'll head to the cannery."

"And the high school," Alex said. He remembered Mary Shadrin stepping out from the darkness, asking him why they needed such a big truck for cleaning up an empty basement. "They probably know we've got food stored there now. Medical supplies, too."

"Connor told me about those assholes who barged into the cannery," Laura said. "I'd bet that's who this is."

"Any chance you'll stay out of this?" Etan said, glancing at his mother. "Maybe at the sheriff's office or somewhere else safe?"

"Etan, son, are you forgetting who first taught *you* how to shoot? If my husband and my sons are going into this mess, I'm not sitting on the sidelines fretting and wringing my hands."

"Maybe you can teach me how to use these rifles when this is over with," Alex said. "At least stay off the front line if you can?"

"We'll see. Go to the cannery first. Someone will tell us where they need help."

Etan had to slow the car as he drove over the steep hill down into Wolf Branch. People were walking everywhere, not nearly enough of them with flashlights so he could avoid them. More than one stepped into the dark street nearly too late.

Alex thought he recognized everyone, but he didn't want to depend on that. Anyone who hadn't been in one of his classes, at the community garden, or at the cannery could be his next door neighbor and he'd have no idea.

The crowd grew thicker the closer they got to the high school. Several cars and pickup trucks were scattered all over the parking lot, and Alex did recognize the people standing around the cannery's locked door. Walt Colley, Linda, Father Price, even Harry Mullins. Alex had never seen him wearing jeans instead of his suit.

He didn't see Connor anywhere.

"We're not ready for something like this," Etan said as he parked. "Everyone's just running scared."

"We'll have to do better," his mother said. "But we don't have time for that right now."

An endless stream of traffic flowed along the road by the high school. Cars, trucks, a few motorcycles. The gap between the headlights wide enough to plunge their eyes back into near-blindness.

The whole town was in a dull roar, everybody within earshot talking or shouting at each other. Alex heard screams and yells from other parts of Wolf Branch, but he couldn't tell where they were coming from in the near darkness. Only a few motion lights scattered among the buildings and the parade of headlights gave off any light.

"Have you seen Connor?" Laura said, walking up to Harry Mullins.

"He got here a few minutes ago, yeah," Harry said. His eyes moved constantly, watching every vehicle and every person prowling around. "He said something about going to check the high school."

"I'll go get him," Alex said, loud enough for only Etan to hear.

"I'm right here." Connor walked across the parking lot from the high school, his hand on the gun at his right hip. He hugged Laura, then stood with his arm around her. "Didn't see anything strange at the school. A couple of people are watching the door now."

"Want to tell me what's going on here, Dad?" Etan said. "Why you came running down here without letting either one of us know?"

Connor looked at Alex, eyebrows raised. Alex shook his head.

"This isn't the time, at least not for that. We'll talk about it when this all settles down. If we can."

A crunching explosion on the other side of town, not far from the hospital, had everyone looking that way. Alex didn't see much light, just a whole lot of noise.

"That's a distraction," he said under his breath, then spoke louder. "They're just trying to distract us."

"Everyone pay attention now!" Harry shouted. Several of the people milling around the cannery were already heading toward the hospital. "Don't follow every god damn false lead they throw us."

The group remaining drew closer, backing toward the cannery. The flow of traffic going by didn't slow in response to the explosion, a disjointed pattern that put Alex even more on edge. Etan grabbed his arm, squeezing hard enough to hurt.

"Something's wrong," he whispered. "Right here, all around us."

Alex saw Connor freeze, staring at the road. He turned and looked at the two of them. He kissed Laura's cheek before he stepped away. He frowned, shook his head, and walked toward the road.

"Get them all behind the building," he said to Etan and Alex. "Take care of her."

"Connor, wait!" Alex said, his voice an intense whisper.

"It's something there, the road," Etan said right into Alex's ear. "I can't see what, but I know it's that way."

"Then we have to stop it," Alex said.

"We don't know what we're trying to stop." Etan's fingers sank into Alex's bicep as he pulled him backward. "I can't see, Alex! Maybe he can!"

"Behind the building!" Connor shouted. "Now!"

Alex saw his silhouette against the headlights turning the corner toward the school.

Then he was gone.

"Connor!" Laura tried to run toward the road.

Etan grabbed her around the waist.

"Everybody back!" he shouted, dragging his mother backward. "Get away from the road!"

"Behind the building!" Alex couldn't see his father-in-law any more. Only that slow line of headlights against the darkness. "Laura, get back!"

He helped Etan with his mother, lifting her off her feet as she screamed into their ears.

"Stop it! Connor! Let me go!"

The others followed, looking around with wide eyes.

One of the big trucks slowed, veering toward the parking lot, the double cab full of people. A man crouched in the back.

The lights shifted. He was gone.

They pushed Laura behind the building.

Alex saw a shadow dart forward. Connor ran alongside the truck.

He reached into the open window of the huge double cab truck.

Shouts from within and from the bed.

The truck jerked away from the cannery, too sharp.

It overturned on the steep road. Metal barrels and what looked like sticks spilled out of the bed.

Alex had one last glimpse of his father-in-law dropping away from the window.

Chapter 34

THE MASSIVE BLAST knocked everyone to the ground.

Etan saw the others in the orange glow, felt heat on his skin. He crawled forward, shaking his head. His ears weren't working.

His mother was still, slumped against the wall, Harry Mullins trying to get to his feet beside her. Linda sat against the building, hands over her ears.

A twisting black hole in the middle of Etan's gut threatened to drag his awareness into the void with his mother.

Someone touched his shoulder.

Alex was on his knees beside him. His mouth moved in the dead silence. Etan staggered to his feet, but Alex blocked his way.

He thought his husband was saying *too hot*. The air felt more brutal than late August in Chicago, but with no humidity to slow the effect. An oily, chemical stench permeated his nose, mouth, and throat.

Etan tried to push forward around the edge of the building again. Alex wrapped both arms around him and pulled him against the cinderblock wall.

Etan watched Alex move his hand around the edge, toward that orange light.

The light his father had died in.

Alex shook his head, then pointed the opposite direction.

His mother was straining against Harry Mullins and Walt Colley, trying to get to the same corner. Her mouth was open wide, her throat bulging, arms outstretched. Etan slipped his own arms around Alex's waist, holding tight before he was ready to help his mother. Both were crying when he finally let go.

Etan and Alex caught Laura Griffith's hands, trying to get her to focus, to pay attention. She twisted and writhed, shaking her head. Etan finally held her face, staring into her eyes from a few inches away.

Her wild gaze softened as she finally saw him. His mother said no, over and over again. Etan caught her before she could hit the asphalt.

Father Price staggered forward and put his arms around Etan, helping support his mother's sagging weight. He bowed his head, his lips moving.

Etan turned away. What god would let a good man like his father die in such a way? And what good did praying do now that it was all over?

Whoever Father Price was trying to reach was as deaf as Etan. Or simply didn't care.

He helped Walt and the priest settle his mother against the side of the building, then turned to look for Alex. He stood at the edge of the building with Harry and Linda, the three of them trying to communicate in broad gestures.

When Alex pointed toward the still-raging fire, a vision ripped through Etan's mind. He grabbed Linda and Alex.

"No!" he shouted, sure they still wouldn't hear him. "More bombs! They haven't exploded yet!"

For the first time in his life, Etan understood why the death masks tormented his grandmother so horribly.

Harry and Linda stared at him, trying to understand.

Both of them screaming, tearing at their flesh burning and torn by shrapnel.

Alex nodded, pulling the other two back.

Alex rolling in agony, unable to stop the chemical fire that devoured the flesh from his bones.

Etan moved behind the three of them and pushed them toward his mother and Father Price, still huddled on the ground.

This time he didn't hear the blasts, five in rapid succession. The ground rumbled under his feet, the orange shadows blazed into daylight. His already tender skin protested at painful levels of heat.

He kept his eyes squeezed closed, not wanting to see the sickening visions again. Gritty fingers on his cheek forced him to look.

Alex's tense features fell into relief, and he pulled Etan into a tight hug. Alex's face smudged and dirty, but no longer melting into slag. Harry and Linda leaned against the wall, covering their mouths against the increasingly noxious air.

Etan dug in his pocket. Even with several of the windows shattered from the first blast, they'd be better off inside the cannery. The basement didn't have any windows at all.

When he moved toward the corner, Alex resisted. Etan held the key up, shaking his head. If there were any more bombs, he didn't feel them coming yet. At least for a few minutes, he thought they were safe.

Stepping around the corner drove that word out of his mind for a long, long time.

Chapter 35

Alex followed Etan, stopping as soon as he cleared the edge of the cannery. His brain rejected the input of his watering eyes, threatening to shut down all activities until he provided something more sensible.

The burning truck was invisible under a thick plume of black smoke, sunken into a crater across the two lane road. Another truck and a car were on fire, one in each lane. Several bodies were scattered along the road and in the parking lot.

Alex didn't have to look closer to know Connor wasn't one of them. He was thankful for that much.

A crowd grew as people followed the light and stench, far worse than the diversion over toward the hospital. A few knelt over more bodies, probably caught in those last explosions.

Etan's hot hand pulled him into the cannery, into blessedly cooler and less polluted air. The window on the other side of the double doors held crazed glass still intact. Alex's engineer mind seized on the chance to assess the damage.

Damage he might actually be able to repair.

The two windows in the small office, closest to the road, were gone. Alex felt glass crunching under his shoes as he closed the door, then looked for some way to block more smoke from getting inside. He wedged several towels under the office door.

Pots and utensils were scattered all over the floor, nearly as grimy as when he'd first set foot inside nearly two years ago. He turned to tell Etan everything looked okay before he remembered his husband wouldn't be able to hear him.

His panic at not seeing Etan died when he walked in, supporting his mother with Linda on the other side. The way his mother-in-law hid her face against her son's chest tore Alex's heart out all over again.

Alex unlocked the basement door, hoping the ventilation system hadn't drawn the foul smoke down there. The emergency lights showed them a dim but clean path. Walt grabbed several bottles of cider from the cooler as he passed by.

The ice-cold liquid made it clear how badly Alex's throat hurt. He wished for something stronger for Laura. He'd settle for not being able to hear her crying, though he hoped that damage wasn't permanent.

His legs gave out and he slowly slid to the floor beside Laura, still leaning against Etan. She gripped Alex's hand without looking up.

Linda started to give Alex a note written on the back of an inventory sheet, then hesitated. He took it with his free hand.

Sandy's outside. At least twenty dead, maybe more later. Trouble seems to have stopped. Still, plenty who live in town offering for folks who live out a ways to stay here tonight or longer.

So sorry. Brave thing he did.

Alex glanced at Laura to make sure she wouldn't see, then handed the note to Etan. His carefully neutral expression didn't change as he read, then nodded.

Linda handed Alex one more note, this one on a tiny sheet torn out of a spiral notebook. He didn't have to ask who this one came from.

Have to head back to the hospital. Like to check all of you over first. S.

Alex nodded, and Linda headed back up the stairs. He showed the note to Etan, then passed it along to Walt and Harry.

Sandy was hardly formal in her medical practice, and tonight she was wearing pink sweatpants and a matching hooded sweatshirt, both as sooty and stained as her hands and face. She pointed to her ear, then to Alex.

When he shook his head, she knelt and shined a bright light with a tiny magnifying glass into his ears. She sat back with a grim smile, scribbled for a few seconds, and showed him the notebook.

No rupture. If not hearing in 24 hrs, will reexamine. Should be fine, tho. Hurt elsewhere? Dizzy? Lose consciousness?

He shook his head again, then got to his feet when she took Laura's hand.

The exams were all the same, except asking all of them to help keep an eye on Laura for concussion. And depression.

Alex stood beside Walt and Harry, all of them glancing at Etan, then each other. Harry finally held out his hand for the notepad.

Sandy showed her answering note to all three of them.

Could certainly use help if you feel up to it. Will take Etan and Laura to my house. You too, Alex. Long as you need to stay.

The fire was out when they got upstairs, and people were covering up the bodies. The whole ones, at least. Alex forced himself to ignore the smaller parts, the bloody ones. Twisted bits of metal and tiny glittering pieces of glass were all over the road and parking lot.

The endless line of traffic was gone with no way to get past, but several vehicles ringed the parking lot with their lights on. The town beyond remained mostly dark.

Sheriff Grant and the deputies helping near the still hot crater stopped when Etan walked by with his mother. She never raised her face, letting him lead her to a waiting van. Etan looked each of them in the eye and nodded.

Walt, Harry, and Linda joined the cleanup. When Alex tried to get into the van, Etan shook his head. He slowly mouthed "You want to stay."

"Your Mom," Alex said, strangely aware of the silent rumble in his own throat and chest.

Etan held up a small pill bottle. He folded both hands under his cheek and closed his eyes. Alex hadn't seen Sandy give it to him.

"Sure?" he said, reaching for Etan's hand. "You okay?"

"Sure. Okay for now." He pointed to himself, then mimed being asleep again. He kissed the back of Alex's hand. "Love you."

Alex held his hand over his heart, watching the van drive away. He felt more relieved than guilty at leaving Etan alone with his mother and with his own grief.

That relief made Alex's guilt worse.

Unbearable pain lurked hot and heavy in his chest. That would probably hit him when he finally could talk to Etan. And Laura. But right now, he held on to knowing the thing he'd been dreading was over. The brief delay in dealing with their loss might help him get through the next few days.

Nothing would make the weeks and months ahead any easier.

By the time he crawled into bed with a deeply sleeping Etan several hours later, Alex was exhausted enough that he didn't need any of the pills on the bedside table.

Chapter 36

Etan gazed around the strange bedroom for several seconds, trying to figure out where he was. Walls covered in pastel flowers, comforter on the bed frilly and pink. Neither their house nor his parents' house was so elaborately decorated. Alex was snoring softly beside him in the narrow bed, though.

His parents.

Etan looked at the bedside table, where a clock covered with plastic flowers and balloons told him it was nearly ten in the morning. A small prescription bottle told him why he'd slept so hard, enough that his left arm was numb.

He saw orange light, felt painful heat. His ears still felt muffled, but he heard his own breathing along with those faint, sweet snores.

His father had died in that explosion.

Etan groaned, turning back toward Alex and his warmth. Connor Griffith had saved all of them, and who knows how many others besides. More than firecrackers or even a simple explosive caused a blast that huge.

And Alex had told him the alternative was all the lights of humanity going out. If his grandmother's dreams, and his own, were true, far more than the population of Wolf Branch owed their lives to Etan's father.

That might make sense someday. Right now the loss was too huge and terrible to contemplate, much less accept.

"Etan?" Alex sounded barely awake. "Can you hear me?"

"Yeah, sweetie. I hear you."

"Thank the gods," he said, turning over and kissing Etan's cheek. "Mine's not quite back to normal, but a hell of a lot better."

"I need to go check on Mom. Get some more sleep."

"No, I'm awake," Alex said. "I left you alone last night. I'm not going to today."

Etan stood up and picked up his clothes from the floor. They really did need to get home just to find something less filthy to wear.

"Mom and I were both asleep a few minutes after we got here. I think today's going to be a lot worse."

Alex moved across the bed and caught Etan's hand.

"I'm so sorry about this. I wish I could have stopped it."

Etan shook his head, not ready to deal with Alex knowing what was coming. A small corner of his broken heart, perhaps still controlled by a shy eleven-year-old with horrible nightmares, wanted to be angry at Alex because he let it happen.

That wasn't fair, not if he was telling the truth about Etan's own dreams and his grandfather's journal.

Alex *did* tell the truth, always, certainly about something so serious. Yet he'd kept this to himself for the last several days of his father's life. That was something else that might make sense later.

"He made his own choice," Etan said. "And he did save a lot of people. Maybe all of us."

The murmur of conversation in the dining room had too many deep voices with Sandy's husband the only other man. Sheriff Grant was there, along with one of his deputies, all around the huge round table with Sandy's two children. Etan's heart sank toward his empty stomach at the way his mother sat, leaning forward with one hand holding her forehead.

His chance to avoid facing this particular reality was already over.

"I normally wouldn't say this, but I hope you're awake because you heard us in here," Sandy said.

She'd changed out of the battered pink sweats into plain green scrubs, but her weariness showed in her voice and the dark circles under her eyes. She poured two cups of coffee from a stainless steel carafe.

"You didn't wake us, but I can hear you just fine," Alex said. He put an arm around his mother-in-law's shoulders, and she hugged him.

"Oh sweetheart, you smell awful," she said with a ghostly smile.

"I can help with that." Sandy's husband stood, herding a little boy and a slightly older little girl in front of him. "Probably not the best fit in the world, but they'll do while I throw what you're wearing in the wash. I'll be back in a minute"

Etan sat beside his mother, settling for a kiss on the cheek. "You okay, Mom?"

"No, hon, I'm not. But I'll keep breathing. Sheriff Grant wants to talk to all of us for a minute."

"I won't take up too much of your time," the sheriff said. "Sandy had a long night and you all have a hard day ahead. There haven't been any more problems, so we think the ringleaders were driving that big truck."

"Same ones who came to the cannery before?" Etan said.

"That's how it's sounding from everyone we've spoken to. Everyone who can talk says they're from Maple Ridge. They didn't even have a grocery store up there in good times, and the road was in pretty bad shape from last winter. They've had trouble finding enough to eat for a long while."

He ran his fingers through his short brown hair, looking everywhere but at Etan or Laura for a few seconds.

"A few people pretty much set up a prison camp over the last couple of months, real nasty business. Told everyone we were stopping food deliveries to that convenience store they had, said that was why it shut down back in the fall. Said we were keeping all their food for ourselves. That's why they were shutting down the power from the wind turbines up there, too. Trying to shake us up while they terrorized their own people. Set up barricades to stop people from leaving, made the roads worse themselves. Once the satellite

TV got taken over for the emergency services, they couldn't get hardly any communication from the outside world that far up in the mountains."

"The ones that came with them last night didn't have much of a choice," Deputy Wiggins said, her face cold and pale. "They were rounded up, promised the first food for their families for a few weeks."

"Most of them are half-starved or worked to the bone," Sandy said. "Desperate to check on their families still left up there more than anything else. I don't think they knew about the bombs."

"No, neither do I," Sheriff Grant said. "Not the big ones. Everyone I've talked to is sick over what happened, they truly are. They had a few noise and smoke bombs to scare people, but it looks like the bed of that truck was full of dynamite and steel cans. Hard to say for sure, but it stinks like diesel fuel and fertilizer. That dynamite had to be ancient. Crazy as the leaders may have been, they never would have driven over those bad roads with such an unstable mess unless they planned to use it. I'm sorry, Mrs. Griffith."

Etan's mother shook her head and sighed.

"I'd rather know Connor died for a reason," she said. "Sounds like he saved a lot more than the few of us standing there."

Etan grabbed Alex's thigh under the table, squeezing hard. The dizziness threatening to pull him out of the chair had nothing to do with the explosion.

A thousand massive gears roared and moved around and inside him, joining up the past and the future.

Alex gripped Etan's hand, returning the squeeze. His own disorientation showed in his blue eyes.

"Thing is, we have to figure out what to do with them," Sandy said. "We kept almost thirty at the hospital overnight, but they can't stay there forever."

"All involved in the raid?" Etan's mother said.

"Yeah, at least all from Maple Ridge," Deputy Wiggins said. "Like Dr. Hughes said, they're all in bad shape, but worried about their folks still up on the mountain."

"Maybe we should take them right back where they came from,"

Alex said under his breath, but everyone around the table heard him. Sheriff Grant broke the long silence.

"A bunch of them told me there are people still left up there. Women and children. Rumors of some men too sick to make it. I feel sick myself that we didn't know what was going on so close by."

"I don't know how bad off they'd have to be to get left behind," Sandy said. "One boy they dragged along has a shattered kneecap, one he got within the last couple of days. Anyone on Maple Ridge won't last long in this cold with worse on the way. Smells like snow outside, and they'll get it worse than we do. The raiders brought all the working vehicles and locked up all the food."

"I figure we have tough choices to make here," the sheriff said. He refilled everyone's coffee cups, not really paying attention to what his hands were doing. "Now and going forward as things get worse out in the world. Do we take folks like this in, or do we try to lock the place up tight?"

Etan swallowed the coffee just as absently, inhaling air across his scorched tongue.

He'd always wondered what Anne's map with the glowing lights looked like. Right now he saw one zoomed in so close that it looked like the view from a helicopter hovering low over Wolf Branch. The contours of mountains and valleys surrounding the town sharp with trees bare for winter.

The small grid of downtown, only a few blocks in either direction, held a few hundred red lights. Some moved down the streets too smoothly to be walking, others clustered together inside the buildings. A larger cluster huddled inside the hospital. A few of those were as pale as the little girl's comforter he and Alex had slept under the night before.

The view shifted, pulled back, and followed the wider two lane heading out of Wolf Branch. The gentle right turn toward Maple Ridge led to a narrow road, twisting as it climbed the steep mountain. A few dozen lights were scattered through the tiny community near the top, almost all of them faded to barely visible.

A few, though, blazed so brightly that his inner eye squinted from the brilliance.

"We've lost how many in the US alone?" he said, focusing on the room again. "Close to fifty million already? And easily three billion worldwide? We all know that's just the beginning. Probably twice that will be gone by the end of this winter, even if we stop hearing about it."

Everyone watched him silently. Only Alex responded with a tiny nod and by squeezing Etan's hand.

"Can we afford to take people back up there to die? Or leave the ones trapped up there to starve to death? We *will* have to protect ourselves from something else like last night. I doubt they'll be the last. But if we forget what we're fighting for, why we're even trying to survive, none of this will be worth it."

Chapter 37

Barely a week later, the Griffiths' house felt like it had been abandoned for years. The floors and walls were clean, and everything was in perfect repair inside and out, just the way Connor had left it. All the large furniture was already moved out, with several people helping out over the last few days.

But even before Alex helped Etan and Laura empty and pack up the last few things, the heart that made it a home was gone.

A pile of boxes waited for them on the broad front porch. Neither he nor Etan had the strength to protest when Laura insisted they take many of Connor's things. Her smaller apartment in town simply wouldn't have room for so much. That sounded like a reasonable argument, until Alex saw the place.

Laura was going to have more room than they did in their house. But again, it was easier to go along.

They were taking a break for one last lunch at the picnic table where they'd shared dinner with Etan's parents, after the awful drive from Chicago. Connor and Evan had built this one around the same time they built the one at Etan and Alex's house. The sun high overhead had melted the last of the snow that fell the day after Connor died, and the fire pit nearby kept them warm enough.

"Is anyone going to move in here, Mom?" Etan said.

"I don't know," Laura said. She looked around, then smiled at Etan. "I hope one of the families from Maple Ridge will, until they get themselves settled. Maybe you two will when you start a family."

Alex met Etan's gaze, expecting the sadness he saw there. He knew children would be in their future, just as well as he knew Etan would take a while to get there while he was awake.

He hadn't yet told Etan about the strong recognition he'd been caught up in during the first rescue trip to Maple Ridge, for one thing. Snow fell up on that mountain as hard as the blizzard the night he'd met Etan back in Chicago. Patterns in that snow led Alex right to two women he knew would be part of their future as surely as he'd known Etan would be part of his.

"I don't know about moving," Etan said. "We love our house. This may not be the best time to be raising kids."

She snorted and rolled her eyes.

"There's never a *best* time for that, not really. Just easier and harder times. Whether you want to think about it this way or not, now is an important time, though. There won't be enough of us left at this rate unless your generation joins in."

"We'll see," Etan said.

"I have to ask one more time, Laura," Alex said. "Are you sure about moving into town? This is really soon to make such a big decision."

"I know, hon. I love the house, and it just feels empty. Like a tomb. Ghosts around every corner. Getting through a winter out here with the power out half the time by myself sounds like a nightmare. I'm not so sure you two should try it this year."

"The power will be a lot more stable now that we can keep an eye on things at Maple Ridge," Alex said. "I've already got electricity set up at our place. The water turbine will keep the basics going even if the wind turbines have trouble, and I'm going to add solar over the next couple of weeks. I could easily do that down here if you want to stay."

She shook her head and patted his arm.

"I appreciate it, Alex, I really do. If someone does move in here, that would be a fine welcome gift. But I'm ready to go."

"Fair enough," Etan said. "The cannery is as good as new, so we'll be helping Sandy with the hospital. Or Alex will. I'm just a hired mule for this kind of thing. If the weather holds, maybe we can get started on your apartment building next."

The three of them finished their sandwiches in silence. Alex was sure he wasn't the only one remembering the first night after they'd arrived from Chicago. Connor and Laura stuffing them full of enough food for at least four people.

He watched the smoke from the fire pit drifting in the cool wind, the changing directions lighting up a warning in the pattern recognition machine in his mind.

"I need to ask you two something," Laura finally said. "It's taken me a couple of days to work up the courage, so just let me get this out." She drummed her fingers on the table, so much like Etan often did. "Did you know what was going to happen to Connor? I'm not asking whether you could have stopped it. I know both of you too well to think you wouldn't have. But did you know?"

Alex looked into his mother-in-law's eyes, wishing he could call a time out and talk to Etan for just a few seconds. He hadn't stopped asking himself whether he could have prevented Connor's death since Etan's first dream about his grandfather's journal.

That question would likely haunt him for the rest of his life.

"We didn't know exactly what would happen," Etan said. He took his mother's hand across the table. Alex held her other one. "I dreamed something was coming, some kind of big change, but I didn't know what it would be."

"That could have been about the raid, too," Alex said, thankful for his husband's lead. "But not clear enough to stop it. I don't know if we could have stopped something that big even if we'd known when it would happen."

"Probably not," Laura said. "Not before we knew what to watch for."

"Exactly," Alex said. "Deputy Wiggins, Melissa, I mean, being able to sense who will cause trouble is going to be a huge help. I'm starting to suspect everyone from Maple Ridge can do the same."

The efforts to welcome everyone had started the night after the raid and hadn't yet slowed. From a huge dinner in the basement of the same church where he and Etan had gotten married, to offers of clothing and shelter, to the new arrivals increasingly asking what they could do to help in their new home.

The country and the world continued to tear themselves apart all around them, but after the one horrible night, Wolf Branch remained calm.

Etan's mother and everyone from both Wolf Branch and Maple Ridge seemed to be channeling their grief and fear into building a new community together.

"There's more talk of organizing the town council again," Laura said, watching Etan instead of Alex. "Harry Mullins, Linda Burns, Father Price. A few people from Maple Ridge. Your new friends Iris and Gena. The two of you would be a welcome addition."

Alex tried to hide his smile. Laura might not be able to see anything unusual about the future, but she retained her full abilities to read her family. She'd recognized Iris and Gena as surely as he had. Etan shook his head, then turned to stare into the fire pit.

"That's not…"

"Safe?" Alex said, remembering the night of the last big meeting. When they'd fled from the riptides and furious energy in the auditorium. And from Mary Shadrin and her followers.

"I hate to admit this, especially to both of you," Etan said, turning back with a faint smile. "It doesn't exactly feel dangerous anymore, no. I'm not ready to jump into anything like that yet. I need to…catch my breath."

When Etan's voice broke, Alex bit back the arguments, persuasion, even the encouragement he had ready. He had his doubts about his mother-in-law making such a huge change so soon after Connor's death. And he'd spent every night since the explosions with Etan held tight, both of them caught in mourning that felt endless and impossible.

He had no doubts that Etan *wasn't* ready for the council or anything else.

Not yet.

"We could all use a little time to catch up," Alex said, rubbing

Etan's back. "Mary isn't in much of a position to cause trouble anymore, but the more people we have who can see what's coming, the better."

"What gets me about Mary is she *does* see what's coming," Etan said. "A form of it, anyway. It's like she gets a warped version, or the people around her twist it. They all stayed away from town that night."

"Sure, because they thought *we* were going to attack *them*," Alex said. He trusted Etan's perception, but he didn't think he'd ever trust Mary. "That wasn't particularly helpful."

"But there was an attack," Laura said. "They had that part right, and by staying away, they stayed safe. To tell you the truth, I don't see how any of you can stand it. Knowing what's coming, even a little bit. I never understood how Anne could, either. Hard as this has been, I'd rather not know."

"Gemaw didn't stand it very well," Etan said. He moved closer to Alex and put an arm around his waist. "Not until she was with Grampa. That makes all the difference."

"Well, I have something I've been wanting to ask you two," Alex said. "That night, that last night, Connor looked toward the road before that truck could have been in sight. He was there before they were, before any of us could have seen anything. Do you think he saw things? Not as often as Etan or Anne, but sometimes?"

"I think he did," Laura said. She rubbed her wedding ring with her thumb. "He was pretty damn confident when we met. And when you two met."

"That much is hereditary," Alex said, smiling at Etan. "We both knew as soon as we met."

"Connor knew I was pregnant with Etan before I did. Same thing when I went into labor. He wasn't the least bit surprised when Etan called to say you two were moving back home."

Alex knew he had to keep his own thoughts about Connor's abilities—and Etan's—to himself for now. Etan wasn't ready to know how much they'd have to be involved in the struggle to keep Wolf Branch safe and strong over the next few years. Not when he was awake, anyway.

The community wasn't as stable as they'd need to be, especially as more survivors straggled in with their own terrors and challenges. Etan's dreams suggested many more would join them over time.

Alex also knew his husband could take a while to adjust to new situations, especially after the terrible shock of losing Connor. But Alex had no doubts that their time on the Council, their future children, all of it would come more easily if he let Etan get there on his own.

He didn't need Etan's dreams or anyone else's to know difficult and dangerous times lay ahead.

For his family, for Wolf Branch, and for the world.

But for the first time since Etan's dreams of the end back in Chicago, Alex's own thoughts of the future were touched with hope.

ABOUT KARI

Kari Kilgore's wanderlust and imagination lead her all over the world on grand adventures. Her heart and family bring her home to her native Appalachian Mountains of Virginia. From that solid base, she and her husband Jason A. Adams bring those adventures to life in fiction.

Kari writes science fiction, fantasy, horror, and contemporary fiction, and she's happiest when she surprises herself. She lives at the end of a long dirt road in the middle of the woods with Jason, various house critters, and wildlife they're better off not knowing more about.

The Confidential Adventure Club

For Kari's exclusive free After The End stories and deleted scenes (including from the Storms of Future Past Series), discounts, early pre-sale releases, adorable pet photos, and a whole lot more not available anywhere else, visit The Confidential Adventure Club at www.smarturl.it/sofp-welcome.

Hope to see you there!

www.karikilgore.com
www.spiralpublishing.net

ALSO BY KARI KILGORE

I hope you enjoyed reading *Joining the Storm* as much as I enjoyed writing it. For more of the Storms of Future Past series, including Book Three, *Into the Storm*, swing by www.smarturl.it/storms-series. Check out more of my fiction at www.karikilgore.com.

The Confidential Adventure Club

Want to read an exclusive short story with Etan's father Connor and his grandfather Evan, from the time between Book One, *Dreaming the Storm,* and *Joining the Storm?*

Want more fiction from Kari, including stories, discounts, and box sets not available anywhere else? Want to hear about locations, research, and other cool things that inspired this story and beyond? All that and adorable pet photos, too?

Join The Confidential Adventure Club and get a thank you gift of *In the Eye of the Storm*, an exclusive short story from The Storms of Future Past Series, and a whole lot more at www.smarturl.it/sofp-welcome.

Hope to see you there!

Novels:

Until Death

The Dream Thief

Dreaming the Storm: Book One of the Storms of Future Past Series

Fighting the Storm: Book Four of the Storms of Future Past Series

Novellas:

Songs in the Mountain

Legacy of the Land

Restricted Species

The Becalmed

In the Pines

Into the Storm: Book Three of the Storms of Future Past Series

Short Stories:

Renovations

Intentions

The Garbage Belt

The Seeds of Love

Wicked Bone

The Sound of Murder

Terminalia

Little Five: A Terminalia Story

Reflections

Collections:

Fantastic Women: A Dark Fantasy Novella Trio

Fantastic Shorts: Volume 1 - A Fantasy Short Story Collection

"Kari Kilgore is an author to watch—her lyrical voice a siren song; her insight, conjured voodoo."

—Richard Thomas, author of *Breaker* and *Tribulations*